"Take your h

For a brief second, something akin to regret glimmered in his expression. But he released her and stepped back. "I'm sorry. I don't usually manhandle women."

She wanted to believe him, but she'd suffered her share of men who did. So she refused to let him off the hook.

His loud exhale punctuated the air. "Please sit down. I'll behave."

He looked so contrite that a tingle of something like respect danced through her. But she refrained from commenting as another image taunted her. One of Ray's hands on her, tenderly stroking her, making her feel safe. No, not safe. Alive.

Fool.

Ray McCullen was anything but safe.

And judging from his brusque attitude, he was going to hate her when he learned the reason for her visit.

ROPING RAY McCULLEN

USA TODAY Bestselling Author

RITA HERRON

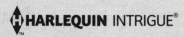

To Sue, who just had her own cowboy adventure!

Recycling programs
for this product may
not exist in your area.

ISBN-13: 978-0-373-74958-4

Roping Ray McCullen

Copyright © 2016 by Rita B. Herron

Printed in U.S.A.

HARLEQUIN®
www.Harlequin.com

USA TODAY bestselling author **Rita Herron** wrote
her first book when she was twelve but didn't think
real people grew up to be writers. Now she writes
so she doesn't have to get a real job. A former
kindergarten teacher and workshop leader, she
traded storytelling to kids for writing romance, and
now she writes romantic comedies and romantic
suspense. Rita lives in Georgia with her family.
She loves to hear from readers, so please visit her
website, ritaherron.com.

Books by Rita Herron

The Heroes of Horseshoe Creek

Lock, Stock and McCullen
McCullen's Secret Son
Roping Ray McCullen

Bucking Bronc Lodge

Certified Cowboy
Cowboy in the Extreme
Cowboy to the Max
Cowboy Cop
Native Cowboy
Ultimate Cowboy

Harlequin Intrigue

Cold Case at Camden Crossing
Cold Case at Carlton's Canyon
Cold Case at Cobra Creek
Cold Case in Cherokee Crossing

Visit the Author Profile page at
Harlequin.com for more titles.

CAST OF CHARACTERS

Ray McCullen—He must find out who's trying to sabotage Horseshoe Creek, but he can't protect his brothers from his father's secret any longer... especially now that Scarlet Lovett, the woman his father thought of as a daughter, is in danger.

Scarlet Lovett—She loved Joe McCullen like a father and now must rely on his son to protect her, but she can't lose her heart to Ray.

Lloyd Pullman—He threatened revenge against Scarlet for taking his child away from him—is he trying to kill her?

Barbara Lowman—Joe McCullen's mistress gave Scarlet a home to appease Joe, but he never married Barbara or took her and Bobby to Horseshoe Creek... is she out for revenge?

Bobby Lowman—Does Joe's illegitimate son hate the McCullens and Scarlet enough to kill them?

Hugh Weatherman—Is he the caring coworker he appears to be?

Arlis Bennett—His cousin went to jail because of the McCullens; is he trying to run them out of business?

Marvin Hardwick and Stanley Romley—Did someone pay these ranch hands to set the barns and ranch house on fire?

Prologue

Ray McCullen hated all the secrets and lies.

He despised his father, Joe McCullen, even more for making him keep them.

In spite of the fact that his brothers, Maddox and Brett, thought he didn't care about them or the family, he had kept his mouth shut to protect them.

God knows the truth about their father had eaten him up inside.

Only now, here he was back at home on the Horseshoe Creek ranch waiting on his father to die, grief gnawing at him. Joe McCullen wasn't the perfect man Maddox and Brett thought he was, but Ray still loved him.

Dammit.

He didn't want to, but the love was just as strong as the hate.

Maddox stood ramrod straight in the hallway outside their father's room, his expression unreadable while Brett visited their dad.

Ray moved from one foot to the other, sweating. He and Brett had both been summoned to the ranch at their father's request—he wanted to talk to each of them before he passed.

Suddenly the door swung open. Brett stalked into the hallway, rubbing at his eyes, then his boots pounded as he jogged down the steps. Maddox arched a brow at him indicating it was Ray's turn, and Ray gritted his teeth and stepped into the room.

The air smelled like sweat and sickness, yet the sight of the familiar oak furniture his father had made by hand tugged at this emotions. His mother had died when he was just a kid, but he could still see her in that bed when he'd been scared at night and his daddy wasn't home, and he'd sneak in and crawl up beside her.

His father's cough jerked him back to reality.

Ray braced himself for a lecture on how disappointed his father was in him—Maddox was the perfect son who'd stayed and run the ranch, and Brett was the big rodeo star who'd accumulated fame and money—while he was the bad seed. The rebel.

The surly one who'd fought with their father, left home and never came back.

"Ray?"

The weak sound of his father's voice forced his feet into motion, and he crossed the room to his father's bedside. God, he didn't want to do thi

"Ray?"

"Yes, Dad, I'm here."

Another cough, pained and wheezy. Then his father held out a shaky hand. Ray's own shook as he touched his father's cold fingers.

He tried to speak, but seeing his father, a big brawny man, so thin and pale was choking him up. Joe McCullen had always been larger than life. And he'd been Ray's hero.

Until that day...

"Thank you for coming, son," his father said in a raw whisper.

"I'm sorry it's like this," he said, and meant it.

His father nodded, but a tear slid down his cheek. "I'm sorry for a lot of things, Ray. For hurting you and your mama."

Ray clenched his jaw to keep his anger at bay.

"I know I put a heavy burden on you a long time ago, and it drove a wedge between the two of us." He hesitated, his breathing labored. "I want you to know that your mama forgave me before we lost her. I...loved her so much, Ray. I hated what I did to her and you."

Grief and pain collected in Ray's soul, burning his chest. "It was a long time ago." Although the hurt still lingered.

"I wish I'd been a better man."

Ray wished he had, too.

"When you find someone special, Ray, love her and don't ever let her go."

Yeah. As if he would ever tie himself down or fall in love. His heart couldn't handle loving someone else to only lose them.

His father coughed, and Ray swallowed hard, the weak sound a reminder that this might be the last time he saw his dad. He wanted to tell him that nothing mattered, that he wasn't ready to let him go yet, that they still had time.

But he'd been called home because they didn't have time.

"The will…" his father murmured. "I tried to do right here, tried to take care of everyone."

Ray tensed. "What do you mean—*everyone*?"

Joe squeezed his hand so tightly, Ray winced. But when he tried to pull away, his father had a lock on his fingers. "Ray, the ranch goes to you boys, but I need you to explain to Maddox and Brett. I owe…"

His voice cracked, his words fading off and he wheezed, gasping for air. A second later, his body convulsed and his eyes widened as if he knew this was his last breath.

"Owe what?" Ray asked. Did he tell Maddox and Brett about his other woman?

"Dad, talk to me," Ray said, panicked.

But his father's eyes rolled back in his head and he convulsed again, his fingers going limp.

Ray jerked his hand free, then rushed toward the door shouting for help. Maddox barreled inside the room and hurried to the bed.

Grief seized Ray as his father's body grew still.

He bolted and ran down the steps, anguish clawing at him.

Damn his father. He'd done it to him again.

Left him holding the secret that could destroy his family forever.

Chapter One

Two weeks later

Scarlet Lovett parked in front of the sign for Horseshoe Creek, a mixture of grief and envy coiling inside her.

This was Joe McCullen's land. His pride and joy. The place where he'd raised his family.

His *real* family. The one with his three beloved sons. Maddox. Brett. Ray.

Maddox was the oldest, the responsible one who was most like Joe in his devotion to Horseshoe Creek. He was also the sheriff of Pistol Whip, Wyoming.

Brett was the handsome, charming bull rider who was most like Joe in his flirtatious smile, his love for women and chasing dreams.

Ray was the youngest, the angry one who looked most like Joe, but he resented his father because he'd walked in on Joe with Barbara and knew about his indiscretion.

Scarlet watched a palomino at the top of a hill in the pasture as it stood alone, seemingly looking down at three horses galloping along together. Just like that lone horse, she had stood on the periphery of the funeral a few days ago, her heart aching, her anguish nearly overwhelming her.

Yet she'd felt like an outsider. She hadn't spoken to the brothers. Had sensed they wouldn't want her to share their grief.

She wasn't part of that family. No, she'd lived with Barbara and Bobby, the *other* family Joe had kept secret.

The one the McCullen boys knew nothing about.

Well…except for Ray. And he didn't know about her or Bobby…just Barbara.

Still, Joe had been the closest thing she'd ever had to a father.

She swiped at a tear, her hands trembling as she unfolded the letter he'd left for her before he'd passed.

My dearest Scarlet,
I was blessed to have sons, but I never had a daughter—until I met you.
    My sweet girl, the moment I saw you in that orphanage and looked into those big, sad, blue eyes, you stole my heart. I admired

your strength, your spunk and your determination to make it in this world, no matter what hard knocks life doled out for you.

You taught me how to be a better man, that family is not all about blood.

I'm sorry I didn't have the courage to tell my sons about you and Barbara and Bobby when I was alive. In my own way, I thought I was protecting them, and protecting the three of you by keeping the two parts of my life separate.

Truthfully, Barbara and I...we were over a long time ago. She knew that and so did I. But I'm trying to do right by all of you now.

If you're reading this, you must have received the envelope I left for you. I have willed you a sum of money to help you make a fresh start, and a piece of ranch land with a small cabin on it for your own home.

Bobby will also receive a share, although you know that he resents me, and he's had his troubles, so I have placed stipulations on his inheritance.

But you...my dear, I know you will use your inheritance to further our work at The Family Farm and help the children, and that you will treasure everything Horseshoe Creek has to offer.

Ranching and living off the land has always been in the McCullen blood, and in our hearts.

Know that you are in my heart, as well.
Love always,
Joe

Scarlet folded the letter again and slipped it inside the envelope, then shifted her Wrangler into Drive and wove down the path to the farmhouse Joe called home.

She wiped at a tear as she parked, and for a moment, she sat and admired the sprawling house with the big porch. It looked so homey and inviting that she could easily picture Joe here with his sons, enjoying family time riding on the land, big dinners over a table piled with homemade food and fishing in Horseshoe Creek.

But she had a bad feeling those sons wouldn't welcome her.

Her stomach twisted at the idea of rejection, and she considered turning around and fleeing. Never contacting the McCullens and claiming what Joe had left her. Disappearing from Pistol Whip and starting over somewhere else.

Barbara and Bobby didn't care about her. No one did.

Except Joe. He'd seen something in her that had inspired her to be a better person.

He'd made her feel loved, as if she was important, when she'd never felt loved or part of a family before.

She looked down at Joe's handwriting again and remembered his words, and opened the door of her vehicle.

Joe had loved her and wanted her to have a piece of his land to remember him by.

She wanted it, too.

Like Joe said, she'd had hard knocks. She was a survivor and a fighter. But she also deserved love and a home.

She took a deep breath, strode up the porch steps to the front door, raised her fist and knocked.

RAY STARED AT the suitcase he'd brought with him when he'd come home, glad he hadn't unpacked.

The itch to leave Horseshoe Creek burned in his belly. The burden of his father's secret was just too damn much.

But the lawyer handling their father's will had been out of town, so they still hadn't dealt with that. And it *would* be something to deal with.

Maddox had also shocked him by asking him and Brett to stand up for him at Maddox's wedding to Rose.

Dammit, seeing his oldest brother happy and in love had done something to him. Not that the brothers had repaired their relationship completely, but two weeks back together on the ranch had mellowed their fighting.

While Maddox and Rose were on their honeymoon, Ray had agreed to oversee the daily running of the ranch. He'd forgotten how much he liked riding and driving cattle.

Brett was busy drawing up plans for the house he and Willow were building for them and their son. They had married in a private ceremony, then moved in to one of the cabins on the property until their dream house was ready. Meanwhile, watching Brett with his little boy, Sam, had stirred up feelings Ray didn't even know he had.

Like envy.

He shifted, uncomfortable with his thoughts. It wasn't as if he wanted to get married or have a family. Not after the way his own had gotten screwed up.

He liked being alone. Liked hanging out in bars, meeting women who demanded nothing from him but a good night of sex. Liked owning his own private investigations business. He could take whatever case he wanted, travel to another state without answering to anyone and come home when he damn well pleased.

It'll all be over soon, he reminded himself. Maddox and Rose would be back in a couple of days.

And so would Darren Bush, the lawyer handling the will.

Of course, if his father had made provisions for

that woman in his will as he'd implied in his private conversation with Ray, the storm would hit.

Maddox and Brett would both be pissed as hell.

Maybe they could pay off the woman and she'd be out of their lives forever.

Then Ray could go back to his own life. Sink himself into a case and forget about family and being the outcast.

The front doorbell dinged, and Ray waited for Mama Mary, the family housekeeper and the woman who'd raised him and his brothers after their mother died, to answer it. But it dinged again, and he remembered she'd made a trip into town for groceries, so he jogged down the stairs.

When he opened the door, he was surprised to see a woman standing on the porch. Instinctively heat stirred in his belly. He didn't know they made women like her in Pistol Whip.

She reminded him so much of those porcelain dolls his mother liked to collect that, for a moment, he couldn't breathe.

She was petite with long, wavy blond hair, huge oval-shaped baby blue eyes and milky white skin. A faint sprinkle of freckles dotted her dainty nose, making her look young and sweet. But that body told a different story. Her curves had been designed for a man's hands.

The wind kicked up, swirling her hair around her heart-shaped face, and she shivered and hunched inside her coat.

"Mr. McCullen?"

He nodded. "Yeah. I'm one of them. Who are you looking for? Maddox? He lives here."

She shrugged. "Actually I'd like to talk to Ray."

Her whisper-soft voice sent his heart into fast motion. "That's me." Did she need a PI?

She shivered again, then glanced in the entryway. "May I come in?"

He realized she was cold and that he'd been staring, and he stepped aside and waved her in. *Good grief.* Women didn't normally cause him to stutter or act like a fool.

But the combination of her beauty and vulnerable expression mesmerized him.

A wary look crossed her face, but she squared her small shoulders and followed him inside to the den. A fire roared in the ancient brick fireplace, the rustic furnishings the same as they had been when Ray lived here years ago.

The manners Mama Mary had instilled in him surfaced. "Would you like some coffee?"

"That would be nice." She clutched a patchwork homemade shoulder bag to her and sank onto the leather sofa in front of the fire.

He walked over to the sideboard in the adjoining dining area where Mama Mary always kept a carafe of hot coffee, then poured two cups.

"Cream or sugar?" he asked.

"Black," she said, surprising him. Half the

women he met wanted that froufrou fancy fla-
vored coffee and creamer.

He handed her the cup and noticed her hand
trembling. She wasn't simply cold. Something
was wrong.

"Now, you wanna tell me what this is about?
Did my receptionist at McCullen Investigations
tell you where I was?"

Again, she looked confused. "No, I didn't realize you were a PI."

Ray claimed the wing chair facing her and
sipped his coffee. So, she wasn't here for a case.
"I don't understand. If you don't need my services, then what?"

She fidgeted. "I don't know how to tell you this,
except just to be up front."

That sounded serious.

"My name is Scarlet Lovett. I knew your father,
Ray. In fact, I knew him pretty well."

Anger instantly shot through Ray. He'd been
thinking how attractive she was, but he'd never
considered that she might have been involved with
his old man.

Well, *hell*, even from the grave, Joe McCullen
kept surprising him. And disappointing…

He hardened his look. "*Damn*, I knew he had
other women, but he was robbing the cradle with
you."

Those big eyes widened. "Oh, *no*, it wasn't
like that."

"He was a two-timing, cheating liar." Ray stood and paced to the fireplace as an image of his father in bed with Scarlet flashed behind his eyes. "How long was it going on?" And what did she want?

"Listen to me," Scarlet said, her voice rising in pitch. "Your father and I were not involved in that way. He was nothing but honorable and kind to me."

Yeah, I bet he was. He turned to her, not bothering to hide his disdain. "So what do you want?"

She set her coffee down and folded her arms. "He told me you were stubborn and resented him, but he didn't say you were a jerk."

Ray angled his head toward her. "You're calling me names. Lady, you don't even know me."

"And you don't know me." Scarlet lifted her chin in defiance. "But if you'd be quiet and listen, I'd like to explain."

Ray's gaze locked with hers, rage and grief and other emotions he couldn't define rolling through him.

The same emotions were mirrored in her own eyes.

Needing something stronger than coffee, he set the mug down, then strode to the bar and poured himself a finger full of scotch.

"I'll have one of those, too," she said.

He bit back a retort and poured her a shot, then carried the glasses back to the fireplace. He handed her the tumbler, then sank into the wing chair and tossed his back in one gulp. "All right. You want me to listen. Say what you have to say, then get the hell out."

SCARLET SHUDDERED AT Ray's harsh tone. She'd seen pictures of him and his brothers, and knew Ray was the formidable one.

He was also the most handsome. Sure Brett was the charmer and Maddox was tough, but something about that dark, mysterious, haunted look in Ray's eyes had drawn her.

Maybe because she understood how anger changed a person. She'd dealt with her own share over the years in the children's home.

But Ray had been lucky enough to have a father who'd wanted him. Even if Joe McCullen hadn't been perfect.

"So, spill it," Ray said. "Why are you here?"

"This was a mistake." She stood, fingers closing over the edge of her bag. "I'll leave."

She started past him, but Ray shot up and grabbed her arm. "No way you're leaving until you tell me what the *hell* is going on."

Her gaze met his, tension vibrating between them. She gave a pointed look at her arm where his fingers held her.

"Take your hands off me."

For a brief second, something akin to regret glimmered in his expression. But he released her and stepped back. "I'm sorry. I don't usually man-handle women."

She wanted to believe him, but she'd met too many men who did. So she refused to let him off the hook.

His loud exhale punctuated the air. "Please sit down. I'll behave."

He looked so contrite that a tingle of something like respect danced through her. But she refrained from commenting as another image taunted her. One of Ray's hands on her, tenderly stroking her, making her feel safe. No, not safe. Alive.

Fool.

Ray McCullen was anything but safe.

And judging from his brusque attitude, he was going to hate her when he learned the reason for her visit.

Chapter Two

Ray struggled to wrangle his temper as Scarlet took a seat again.

When he looked at her, he couldn't help but think about those damn dolls his mother had loved so much.

Just like them, she was almost too beautiful to be real.

Like them, she looked fragile, like a piece of china that could break if you held it too hard.

Yet she'd stood up to him and had a stubborn set to her chin that made him suspect there was more to her than surface beauty.

He could easily see why his father might have been attracted to her. But *God*…she was so young…

"I realize what I'm going to tell you may come as a shock," she said softly, "but it's what Joe wanted."

"How do you know what my father wanted?"

Her eyes flickered with uneasiness at his tone. "I told you that I knew him pretty well."

"So you said. But *how* did you know him? Was he your sugar daddy?"

Scarlet sucked in a harsh breath. "No. It wasn't like that, Ray. I met him at The Family Farm outside Laramie."

"The Family Farm?"

Scarlet nodded. "It's a home for children without parents, an orphanage. Your father volunteered there. I was ten at the time we met, but he took me under his wing."

For a moment, Ray couldn't respond. "I find it hard to imagine my father volunteering with children," he finally said. "He was a rancher. He worked the land."

Scarlet shrugged. "He told me once that he had to find a way to atone for his sins. That he hadn't always been the father he wanted to be, and he hoped giving back to some children without families would help make up for it."

Ray's dark gaze met hers, probing, skeptical. "He told you about Horseshoe Creek? About us?"

"Yes," Scarlet said softly. "He loved you and Maddox and Brett. He was proud of all of you."

Ray chuckled, but the sound was filled with sarcasm. "He was proud of Maddox. And maybe Brett because of the bull riding. But he didn't give a damn about me."

"That's not true," Scarlet said. "He loved you

and hated what he did to you. That you knew his flaws."

"That I did." Ray made no attempt to hide his animosity. "He cheated on my mother with some woman named Barbara. But my mother loved him anyway."

Scarlet looked away for a second, which made him even more uneasy.

Her fingers tightened around the strap of that worn-out shoulder bag. "I'm sorry, Ray, I didn't come here to dredge up bad memories."

"My father just died, Scarlet. Coming home already did that." He exhaled. "So why did you come here? To tell me Dad did volunteer work?"

"Not just that, but to tell you what he did for me. I was alone and no one wanted to adopt me. But he gave me a home and a family."

A bead of perspiration trickled down Ray's neck. "What are you talking about?"

"He took me home to live with Barbara and Bobby. Their last name is Lowman."

"You lived with my father's mistress?"

She nodded. "For a while. With her and her son." She hesitated. "Their son."

Her words echoed in Ray's mind as if he'd fallen into a wind tunnel. "*Their* son?"

Scarlet nodded. "I'm sorry. I…thought he was going to tell you about Bobby before he passed."

A deep sense of betrayal cut through Ray,

and he balled his hands into fists. He wanted to punch something.

He had known about the affair, but not that his father had another son.

SCARLET'S HEART SQUEEZED at the pain and shock on Ray's face. She didn't want to hurt this family, only to honor Joe's last wishes.

Ray raked a hand through his thick, dark hair, then walked over to the bar and poured himself another shot. He kept his back to her as he stared into the fire, his shoulders rigid.

She glanced around the living room, absorbing its warmth, giving Ray time to process what she'd told him.

She tried to put herself in his place, to understand how he must feel. Her grief over Joe's death was almost unbearable, and she wasn't even Joe's biological family.

She'd always looked up to Joe for the time he'd donated to the children's home, and had secretly hoped to meet his sons one day, sons that he took pride in and had talked about when Bobby wasn't around.

Joe and Bobby had a tumultuous relationship. Barbara and Joe had kept an on-again-off-again relationship over the years, but Joe had never married Barbara. He'd also been in and out of Bobby's life, partly by choice, partly due to Barbara's moody behavior.

But Joe had admitted to Scarlet once that he'd always loved his wife. No one could ever replace her.

In some ways, Bobby had a right to resent Ray, Maddox and Brett. Although Joe had financially supported him and Barbara, he'd never taken them to his ranch. Even after he lost his wife, he hadn't shared Bobby with his other three sons.

"So I have a half brother?" Finally Ray turned toward her, a harshness in his eyes. "How old is he?"

"Twenty-six," Scarlet said.

"Just a little younger than me," Ray muttered. "Damn my daddy. Even in death, he found a way to screw us."

"I'm sorry, Ray." Scarlet fidgeted. "I know this is a shock. Maybe I shouldn't have come, but—"

"But you did come," Ray snapped. "Because you and Bobby want something? What? Part of Daddy's money? The ranch?"

Scarlet flinched at his accusatory tone. Although she reminded herself that she'd just dropped a bombshell on Ray at a time when he was grieving. Lashing out was a natural reaction.

But Joe McCullen's words in that heartfelt letter echoed in her head. She had loved Joe, and even though he'd made mistakes in his life, he'd cared about her.

Ray must have read her silence as a yes. "That's it, isn't it? You want part of Horseshoe Creek?"

"Ray, please," Scarlet said, her voice quivering. "It's not like that."

Ray's jaw tightened. "Then how is it? You simply came to tell me you're sorry my father is gone? That he has another son, but that he doesn't want part of Dad's legacy?"

Actually Bobby *would* want part of it. And Joe had made arrangements for him, only there were stipulations attached to it. She didn't know what those stipulations entailed, but whatever they were, Bobby would balk.

"I won't lie to you, Ray. I am here because your father left me something." She pulled the letter from her bag. "I had no idea he'd included me or Bobby in his will, but he did. A lawyer named Bush contacted me about the reading."

"Just as I thought," Ray said, animosity dripping from every word.

Self-preservation kicked in. "Listen, Ray, I didn't ask for this. And I don't think Bobby even knows yet. He and Joe didn't get along, and Bobby's had problems in the past, so I don't know what to expect from him now." She shoved the letter toward Ray. "Just read this letter your father wrote me."

Ray's dark gaze latched with hers, tension stretching between them, filled with distrust.

Her hand trembled as she waited for Ray to take the letter. When he snatched it, she finally released the breath she'd been holding, sank back in the chair and struggled to calm her nerves.

But the sight of Ray's big, tough masculine profile haloed by the orange and yellow firelight aroused feminine desires that she'd never felt. Desires that she had no right to feel for the man in front of her.

Desires that couldn't lead to anything.

But something about his strong jaw, that heavy five o'clock shadow and the intensity in his eyes reminded her of Joe. Joe, the man who'd been like a father to her.

Joe who'd sent her here to meet his sons.

She clutched her drink glass again and sipped it. The warm scotch slid down her throat, warming her. Yet the alcohol also reminded her of Joe.

Why had he put her in this awkward position?

He had to have known that Ray and his brothers wouldn't welcome her or want to share any part of their family ranch. That they would be angry, and that the truth would turn their world upside down.

RAY LEANED AGAINST the hearth as he studied the paper Scarlet had handed him. It appeared to be a handwritten letter to her.

In his father's handwriting.

My dearest Scarlet,
I was blessed to have sons. But I never had a daughter—until I met you.

That first line knocked the breath from his lungs. But he forced himself to read further.

By the time he finished, his gut was churning. These were his father's words. His father's sentiments.

Betrayal splintered through him.

Scarlet wasn't lying. His father had loved her, had lead a life that he'd kept from his sons.

What were Maddox and Brett going to say? They didn't even know about Barbara...

"I realize this is a shock to you," Scarlet said softly. "It was to me, too."

Still suspicious though, Ray narrowed his eyes, determined to see the truth beneath the pretty exterior. She was dressed in jeans and a denim shirt, boots, her long blond hair natural, and she wore little makeup or jewelry.

Not his idea of what a gold digger would look like.

But who was to say she hadn't conned his father into writing this when he was ill or on medication?

He'd worked as a PI long enough to know that con artists came in all shapes and sizes, that sometimes the most charming, alluring face hid a devious side beneath.

Scarlet had grown up in an orphanage. Wasn't it common for children who grew up without parents or in troubled homes to have mental problems? Maybe she wanted a family so badly that she'd latched on to his father and had taken advantage of him in a weak moment and convinced him to take her in.

He cleared his throat. He needed more information before he showed this to his brothers. "Where did you get this letter?"

"It came registered yesterday." She gestured toward the envelope. "You can see the return address on the envelope."

Ray hadn't paid attention to it, but he flipped the envelope over and noted the name of a law office. Bush Law, Darren Bush, attorney-at-law.

Darren Bush was his father's lawyer. So she hadn't lied about that.

"You realize I'll need to make sure this is legitimate."

Scarlet bit down on her lower lip. "Yes, but… I'd like the letter back. It's the last thing Joe ever wrote to me."

He clenched his jaw. "He wrote you other letters?"

Scarlet shrugged. "Not letters, but he gave me cards for encouragement when I lived at The Family Farm. And then on birthdays."

Resentment bubbled inside Ray. Why had his father treated her so special when he'd ignored him?

Because you knew what he did to your mother. And his anger and bitterness had driven a wedge between the two of them.

But *dammit*, his father could have tried.

"I'm sorry I upset you," Scarlet said. "I almost didn't come. But—"

"But you did," Ray said again.

"Yes," she said in a voice that cracked with emotion. "I don't want the money per se, but I admired Joe and having a piece of the ranch that he cherished means I'll always have a part of him. I know you and your brothers feel the same way."

Except they were Joe McCullen's blood. And she was…not family at all.

Although according to that letter, his father had loved her like a daughter.

Ray wished to hell he knew exactly how much money and land his father was talking about. And what about this half brother?

The letter mentioned that he had problems. Would he make trouble for the McCullens?

Chapter Three

Scarlet sensed it was time to leave. She hadn't expected the visit to go well, but she'd hoped…

What? That the McCullen men would welcome her into their family as Joe had?

They didn't even know her. Besides, according to Joe, the three brothers had their own differences to work out. Throwing a surprise half brother in the mix that they were unaware of and adding her—who was not even blood kin—had to rock their foundations.

They might even find some loophole to prevent her from receiving what Joe had intended her to have.

A pang hit her. If that happened, she'd live with it. Lord knows, she'd handled rejection before.

Truthfully, she wasn't even sure Barbara had ever wanted her.

At first she'd welcomed her as the daughter she'd never had, but later, Scarlet suspected Barbara had only tolerated her because she thought it might help her win Joe back.

And Bobby… He'd hated her from the beginning.

She stood, Ray's tormented expression tearing at her heart. "I really am sorry about just showing up. I wish Joe had told you about us."

"He was a coward," Ray said.

She bit her tongue to keep from agreeing. Even thinking that made her feel disloyal for all Joe had done for her. But she'd been hurt that her own mother had abandoned her when she was little, and she didn't understand why Joe had allowed his deception to continue for so long.

He had put Ray in a bad spot and left him harboring a secret that must have hurt him terribly.

"He said he wanted to protect your brothers," Scarlet said. "He hated disappointing you all."

"Don't defend him, Scarlet."

"I'm not defending him," Scarlet said. "But everyone makes mistakes, Ray."

Ray's frown deepened, making his eyes look haunted. "I'll call the lawyer and talk to him about this, but for now, I think you'd better go."

So much for making friends with Ray.

No wonder he and Joe had butted heads. They were both stubborn and hardheaded.

He gestured at the door, and she walked toward the entranceway. This old farmhouse had been in the family forever, Joe had said. It was homey and warm. The pictures of the landscape and horses on the walls showcased life on the ranch.

A family portrait of Joe, his wife and the three boys when they were little hung in the hallway like a shrine to the McCullens.

As a little girl, she'd been so alone when her mother had abandoned her. She'd lived on the streets for a few days with a homeless woman. She'd slept in alleys and deserted barns and eaten garbage.

Then she'd gotten sick and the old woman had pushed her into a nearby church with a note saying she had no home and needed help.

She'd developed rheumatic fever, and her heart had been weakened from her illness, making matters worse. No one had wanted to adopt a sick child, so she'd ended up at the children's home.

Ray opened the door and a gust of cold air blasted her, sending a shiver through her. She clutched her shawl around her shoulders and held her head up high.

She'd been called names, ostracized from social situations and left out of sports because she'd been small, sickly and poor.

She wasn't sickly anymore, and she didn't intimidate easily. Joe had taught her to respect herself and fight for what she wanted out of life.

She wanted a family of her own someday.

She'd hoped to be part of this one. But that didn't look as if it would happen.

So she hugged her shawl around her and ran to her Wrangler. Even if the McCullen men didn't want her in their lives, their father would forever live in her heart.

RAY IGNORED THE guilt stabbing at him for his rude behavior with Scarlet.

When people died, especially people who owned land or money, predators crawled out of the woodwork wanting a piece of the pie.

He had to investigate Scarlet and her claims. But if she was telling the truth about there being a half brother, then he and Maddox and Brett would have to deal with the fallout.

And there would be fallout. Especially if their father had left him part of Horseshoe Creek.

He watched the woman disappear down the drive, his throat thickening with mixed emotions. If his father had volunteered at this children's home and cared for her, it meant that he hadn't been the cold bastard Ray believed him to be.

Yet...how could he have lived such different lives? Two families...

After his mother's death, Ray had wondered if his father would marry that other woman. Barbara.

When he'd remained single, Ray had wondered why.

He still wondered.

He scanned the long driveway. Would Barbara show up next?

Wind swirled leaves inside the front door, and he realized Scarlet was long gone, so he shut the door. What the hell was he going to do now?

The furnace rumbled, the sound of wood popping in the fireplace, and he strode back to the living room and studied the family picture on the mantel.

The smiling faces mocked him. They looked like the perfect family.

But the picture was a lie.

Joe had another side to him. He'd slept with this woman Barbara and had a son with her.

And Scarlet...she was the wild card. The stranger he'd given a home to make amends for the mess he'd made.

Ray rolled his hands into fists. He had to find out the truth before the reading of the will.

Dammit, Dad, I'm still covering for you, aren't I?

Yeah, he was. But he hated to destroy his brothers' worlds if he could protect them. After all, Maddox and Brett had both just married.

Brett had been the womanizer, but he'd sowed his oats, and he wouldn't be a cheater like his old man.

One reason Ray had never gotten serious with a woman. If his old man hadn't been able to handle commitment, how could he?

He pulled his phone from his jacket, punched in Bush's number and left a voice mail.

"This is Ray McCullen. A woman named Scarlet Lovett paid me a visit and claims my father left her some money and land. She also claims my father had another son who is a beneficiary. My brothers don't know anything about this yet, and I want to be prepared, so I need to talk you to *before* the reading of the will. Call me as soon as you get this message."

An image of abandoned children living in a group home taunted him and made his gut squeeze with guilt. If Scarlet's story was true, he'd be a bastard to contest his father's wishes.

He grabbed his Stetson and headed outside. He'd drop by that group home and find out for himself.

SCARLET HELD HERSELF together until she reached the edge of the McCullen ranch, but she was trembling so hard by then she had to pull over. She parked beside a sawtooth oak and studied the sign for Horseshoe Creek, then gazed at the beautiful rolling pastures and the rocky terrain in the distance.

Joe had regaled her with stories about raising cattle and working with his sons on the ranch, and about cattle drives and branding in the spring. He'd had big dreams of expanding the horse side of the operation, but when Ray and Brett left Pistol Whip, he and Maddox couldn't handle expansion without them.

The sun was setting, painting the ridges of the mountains beyond a golden hue and the sky a radiant red and orange. Cattle grazed in the pasture to the east, and horses galloped near a stable to the west.

She understood why Joe had loved this land.

And why his sons would want to hold on to it.

Tears trickled down her cheeks. Ray and his brothers were still mourning their father.

So was she. But just like the rest of her life, she had to do it alone. She'd kept her distance at the funeral for fear someone would ask about her relationship with Joe. Plus, she'd respected him too much to intrude on his sons' day.

Maybe she should just disappear from the McCullens' lives now. Forget the will reading. Not ask for anything.

She had her memories of Joe. That was all she needed.

She started her engine and headed back toward her rental house.

She had survived being abandoned as a child, and now she'd earned her degree in social work and was helping other children like herself. She had a fulfilling job and she was giving back.

Even if she was alone at night, it didn't matter. There were children who depended on her.

She wouldn't let them down just like Joe hadn't let her down.

Her stomach twisted. Which meant she couldn't run from the McCullens.

She needed the money Joe had left her to help The Family Farm.

RAY STUDIED THE sign for the children's home— The Family Farm. The house was set back on several acres with room for livestock and stables, but he didn't see any cattle or horses.

He maneuvered the drive and parked in front of the rustic wooden structure that reminded him more of a fishing lodge than a home for children.

Someone had probably designed it that way. *Smart.*

A big front porch overlooked the property, the two-story house more welcoming than he'd expected. A van was parked to the side with an emblem of a circle of children holding hands and the name painted on the side. Two other vehicles were parked in the graveled lot. Probably employees.

He climbed out and walked up the steps, then knocked. A pudgy middle-aged woman with a short brown bob answered the door. "Yes?"

"My name is Ray."

"Faye Gideon," the woman said with a warm smile. "What can I do for you?"

"May I come in and talk to you?"

A slightly wary expression flickered in her

eyes, and she wiped her hands on a kitchen towel. "It's dinnertime for the kids. What's this about?"

He didn't want to divulge that he was a private investigator yet. "I recently met a woman named Scarlet Lovett. She said she grew up here."

Faye's eyes widened, but a smile flitted across her face. "Yes, Scarlet. She did live here. Now she's a social worker and helps place kids in forever homes when she can." She opened the door and stepped onto the porch. "What did you say your name was?"

"Ray McCullen."

She pressed her hands to her cheeks. "Oh, my goodness, I thought you looked familiar. You're one of Joe's boys, aren't you?"

Ray swallowed. "Yes, ma'am. You knew my father?"

"Of course!" Faye grinned. "He volunteered here. That's how he connected with Scarlet. But if you've met her, you probably know all of this."

So Scarlet's story was true.

"I'm so sorry about your daddy," Faye said. "We all loved him. He was so wonderful with the children. We used to be in this old house nearer to town, but it was small and run-down, and Joe helped us build this place. Now we have twelve rooms, a big kitchen and land for the children to run and play."

Ray couldn't believe what she was saying. This

wasn't the man he remembered from his high school years at home.

"We're all sad that he passed and will miss him," Faye said. "Do you want to meet the children? They'll be thrilled to visit with one of Joe's sons. He talked about the three of you all the time."

Emotions welled in Ray's throat. Why hadn't his father told him about this place? About what he was doing?

Because you left and never came back. You refused to talk to him.

And now it was too late.

SCARLET PARKED AT her rental house outside Pistol Whip, still shaken over the conversation with Ray McCullen. But there was nothing she could do tonight except give him time to process the bombshell she'd dropped on him.

Heart heavy, she let herself inside the tiny house. Although it was small, she had filled it with homey furniture, handmade quilts and crafts from Vintage Treasures, and she'd hung photographs of the farmland where the orphanage was housed on the walls.

She loved the beautiful landscapes and had been excited about Joe's plans to add a stable and horses so the children could learn to ride. He'd also intended to add farm animals and assign the children chores to teach them responsibility.

Working together would make them feel like a real family. God knows, most of them were plagued with self-doubt, insecurities and emotional issues.

She lit a fire in her fireplace, brewed a cup of tea, then grabbed her files and spread them on the kitchen table. She was most worried about one of the preteen boys, Trenton Akers. He was angry and lashing out at everyone, which made it more difficult to find him a forever home.

But there was a four-year-old, Corey Case, who a couple from Cheyenne were interested in. She opened the file on the couple to study their background check, but a noise outside startled her.

She went to the back door and peeked through the window in the laundry room. Wind hurled leaves across the backyard that jutted up to the woods. Night was setting in, the gray skies gloomy with shadows.

Suddenly she heard the doorknob jiggle, and she crept to the back door. A second later, the door burst open and Bobby appeared. He'd always been a foot taller than her, but he'd gained at least twenty pounds, making him twice her size.

Her lungs squeezed for air at the fury radiating from him. Beard stubble covered his face, and he reeked of alcohol and cigarettes. "Hello, sis. We have to talk."

Scarlet inhaled sharply. "Bobby, you're drunk. Come back when you're sober."

He gripped her arm, then dragged her toward

the living room and shoved her against the wall. "No, Scarlet. We're going to talk now."

Fear crawled through her. She'd borne the brunt of Bobby's temper before, and barely survived it.

No telling what he'd do now that Joe wasn't around to protect her.

Chapter Four

Ray reluctantly stepped inside The Family Farm house.

Part of him wanted to deny everything Faye was telling him, go home and forget about Scarlet Lovett.

But he couldn't forget about her. Not if his father had included her and this other son in his will.

Bobby Lowman—his half brother.

Good God…he still couldn't believe it. His father had another son. One he and Maddox and Brett had known nothing about.

Maddox and Brett were going to have a fit.

As he scanned the interior of the farmhouse, he couldn't deny his father's influence. It reminded him of the house on Horseshoe Creek. Wood floors, sturdy oak furniture, a giant family table in the dining room, a kitchen adjoining it that held another big round wooden table and a butcher-block counter.

Landscape paintings and farm and ranch tools decorated the walls in the hall and the dining room where several kids of varying ages sat eating what smelled like homemade chicken potpie.

A brick fireplace in the dining room and another one in the living room added to the homey feel.

Laughter, chatter and teasing rumbled from the table.

"I told you it was dinnertime," Faye said. "The kids take turns helping prepare the meal and cleaning up. Their rooms are down the hall. We have a maximum of four children to a room, and in some cases only two. Boys and girls are housed on opposite sides of the main living area."

She escorted him past the dining room to a large room equipped with several smaller tables and a computer area. "The children attend public school, and after school gather here to do their homework. We have volunteers who tutor those who need it."

Ray nodded, trying to imagine his father in this place. "My father tutored kids?"

"No, he said schooling wasn't his forte."

You could say that again.

"But he helped in other ways. He organized games for the kids, like horseshoes, roping contests and, twice a month, he brought a couple of horses over to teach the children grooming skills and how to ride."

She gestured at a back window that offered a view of the pastureland. "He planned to build a stable so we could house a few horses on-site. When the older boys discovered his son was a bull rider, they begged him to bring him here to meet them."

Ray shifted. "That would have required him to tell us about this place."

Faye's eyes flickered with compassion. "I never quite understood that, but I figured it wasn't my place to question your daddy, not when he was doing so much for us."

Hurt swelled inside Ray. Nice that he'd been a hero for these strangers when he'd lied to his own sons.

A little boy with brown hair and big clunky glasses ran in. "Miss Faye, we're done. Barry wants to know if we can go out and play horseshoes."

Faye ruffled the little boy's hair. "I'll be right there, Corey. You guys help Miss Lois clean up now."

Corey bobbed his head up and down, then ran back to the dining room. Ray heard him shouting that they could play once they cleaned up.

Faye squeezed Ray's arm. "You're welcome to stay and play a game with the children. They'd like it, especially since you're Joe's son."

Ray chewed the inside of his cheek. The air was

suddenly choking him. "I'm sorry, I can't today. I have to go."

Faye nodded as if she understood, but her smile was sad. "I don't know what we're going to do now without Joe."

Ray didn't, either. But it wasn't his problem. *Was it?*

Hell, if his father had made provisions for Scarlet and his illegitimate son Bobby, he'd probably made arrangements to take care of this place, too.

Another thing to discuss with the lawyer and his brothers.

He ignored the chatter and laughter in the dining room as he walked past it to the front door. When he made it outside, he inhaled the crisp cool air, but his stomach was churning.

He checked his phone, hoping Bush would return his call, but there were no messages. He had to find out if Bobby planned to attend the meeting and stake his claim.

Ray gritted his teeth. He'd kept the truth from his brothers long enough. They deserved a heads-up before their world fell apart.

He would tell them as soon as Maddox returned.

SCARLET TRIED TO gauge the distance between the couch and the bedroom where she kept the pistol Joe had given her.

He'd insisted she take self-defense classes and

he'd taught her to shoot so she could protect herself. Unarmed, she was no match for a two-hundred-and-forty-pound angry, drunk man.

Knowing Bobby's triggers, that he liked to bully women and that he had no tolerance for people who crossed him, she forced her tone to remain calm. "What do you want, Bobby?"

"I want what's mine." He glared at her, then folded his arms and planted himself in front of her, legs apart on either side of hers, trapping her.

"I understand that and you deserve it."

Distrust radiated from his every pore. "You went to the old man's funeral?"

A pang of grief swelled inside Scarlet. "Yes, but I just watched from the sidelines." She lifted her chin. "I didn't see you there."

"Barbara talked me out of it." He gave a sarcastic chuckle. "I belonged there more than you did. You weren't family."

Scarlet bit her tongue but his hate-filled words hit home, resurrecting old hurts. "I figured it wasn't the time to introduce myself to the McCullen brothers."

It hadn't gone very well today, either.

Bobby removed a pack of matches from his pocket, and she barely resisted a flinch. Bobby had always liked setting things on fire.

He struck a match, lit it and held it in front of her, the orange glow flickering and throwing off heat as he moved it nearer to her face. "I should have been a McCullen," he said, a feral gleam to his eyes. "I should have had everything they did. That big damn ranch house and horses and land and…the privileges that came with it." The match was burning down, and he dropped it in a coffee cup on her table, then lit another and waved it in front of her eyes.

With one beefy hand, he shoved her into a chair. "Then he brought *you* home and treated you like you were his own kid."

Scarlet struggled to keep her breathing steady when she wanted to make a run for it. If she could reach her car, she could escape. And do what?

Call the police. She didn't want to, but she would if necessary to protect herself. "He felt sorry for me, that was all."

His intense look made her pulse hammer. "He gave you more love than he did me."

"That's because you wouldn't let him love you," Scarlet said. "You were always angry, acting out."

"I had a right to be mad. He cheated me out of his name and that ranch." The flame flickered low, nearly burning out, and he suddenly dropped the match into her lap. Scarlet shrieked as heat seared her thigh through her skirt, and she raked the match to the floor, then stomped it out with her boot.

Bobby's maniacal laughter echoed through the room. He grabbed her arm and hauled her to a standing position.

Scarlet sensed the situation was spiraling out of control. She had been a punching bag before and swore she would never be one again.

"Maybe he did when he was alive," Scarlet said as she yanked her arm away. "But he didn't forget you, Bobby. He left you something in his will."

Bobby's eyes widened in disbelief. "What are you talking about?"

"Didn't you receive a notice from his lawyer?" Not that she wanted to tell Bobby about it, but she had to do something to defuse the situation.

His bloodshot eyes pierced her. "His lawyer?"

"Yes," Scarlet said, desperate. "I received a notice to attend the reading." She extricated herself from Bobby's grip. "Let me get it and show it to you. He took care of you in his will, too. Maybe Barbara got the notice."

Bobby cursed, but he allowed her to pass. She heard him in the kitchen digging through her refrigerator, and she rushed to her nightstand. She yanked out her pistol, reminding herself that she couldn't allow him to turn it around and use it on her.

She loaded it, then held it down by her side as she slowly walked back to the den.

Bobby popped the top on a beer as he stepped into the doorway, and she raised the gun and pointed it at him. "I want you to leave."

"You bitch." He started toward her, one fist

knotted as if he planned to slug her, but she lifted the gun toward his chest.

Bobby froze, his jaw twitching. "You were lying about the lawyer and the will."

"No, I wasn't. Ask Barbara. We're all supposed to attend the reading."

Bobby hesitated, still contemplating what she'd said as if he thought she was trying to trick him. "What is this lawyer's name?"

"Darren Bush." Scarlet took a step toward him, her hand steady. "I don't want to use this, Bobby, but I will if I have to. Now, I don't have anything you want here. No money. Nothing of Joe's. And if you want to collect on whatever inheritance he left you, then you need to leave me alone or I'll either shoot you or have you arrested."

Pure rage flashed in his eyes, but he lifted the beer as if to toast her. "Shoot me and you'll go to jail."

"Make one more move, Bobby, and with your record, all I'll have to do is claim self-defense."

Bobby stared at her for a long tension-filled minute, his fury a palpable force. Then he downed the beer, crushed the can in his hand and threw the can at the fireplace. His boots pounded the floor as he strode to the door.

Her hand was shaking as he paused and turned back to face her. "You're going to be sorry for pulling a gun on me."

His evil laugh rent the air as he opened the

door and stormed outside. As soon as the door slammed shut, her adrenaline waned, and she stumbled back to the couch.

Bobby didn't make empty threats.

He would be back for revenge. It was just a matter of time.

RAY PLANTED HIMSELF on a barstool at The Silver Bullet and ordered a beer. Tonight the place was packed, the country music was rocking, the dance floor was crowded and the women were on the prowl.

He tipped his hat at a brunette who'd been eyeing him ever since he walked in, then dropped his gaze to his beer. He had too many problems to even think about crawling into bed with a woman tonight.

Besides, another woman's face haunted him.

Scarlet Lovett's. He couldn't shake their conversation. Worse, he couldn't erase the image of her porcelain face with those damn blue eyes that reminded him of his mother's dolls.

Had his father seen that similarity? Was that the reason he'd been drawn to help Scarlet?

A brawny man with a beard and cowboy hat straddled the stool beside him, then angled himself toward Ray.

"You're one of Joe's sons, aren't you?"

Ray swallowed hard. He'd forgotten what it was like to live in a small town where everyone knew everyone else. And Joe McCullen had been well-known around the ranching community.

"Yeah, I'm Ray."

"Arlis Bennett," the man said. "I'm out at the Circle T."

Ray rubbed his chin. The owner of that ranch, Boyle Gates, had been arrested for his involvement in a cattle-rustling ring.

"I'm planning to expand," Bennett said. "If you and your brothers decide to sell, give me a call." He removed a business card from his pocket and laid it on the bar.

Ray slid it back toward him. "We're not interested in selling. My brother Maddox plans to keep it a working ranch. And my brother Brett is staying to help."

Bennett tossed back his shot of whiskey with a nod. "Well, I just thought you guys might want to move on. That it might be too hard for you to stick around without your father."

Ray shifted, uncomfortable. "It is difficult, but the McCullens have put too much blood, sweat and tears into Horseshoe Creek to ever sell."

"Then I guess we'll be neighbors." Bennett stood and extended his hand. "Nice to meet you, Ray. Again, I'm sorry about your daddy."

Ray nodded and shook the man's hand. But something about the dark gleam in Bennett's eyes reminded Ray of a predator. Not that he should be surprised that someone wanted to buy the ranch.

There might be more offers down the road.

A buxom blonde brushed up against his arm, her eyes glittering with invitation. "Hey, cowboy. Are you lonesome tonight?"

Hell, yeah he was, but an image of Scarlet taunted him. He saw her beneath him in bed, naked and clutching him, that porcelain skin glowing with passion.

"Sorry, honey, I've got to go." He threw some cash on the counter to pay for the beer, then strode toward the door, disgusted with himself for being attracted to the damn woman. She was going to wreck his family.

A gust of wind blasted him as he walked to his Range Rover, and he jumped inside, started the engine and drove to the ranch.

Just as he approached, he spotted smoke billowing in a cloud from the pastureland on the east side.

He cursed. Hopefully it was nothing but a little brush fire, but he accelerated, taking the curve too fast, tires screeching as he neared Horseshoe Creek.

The miles seemed to take forever, his heart racing with each one. Instead of the smoke dying down, it grew thicker, rolling across the sky, orange-and-red flames shooting upward.

He grabbed his phone and punched 911, praying the fire department could get there fast.

The winds picked up and the fire was spreading, eating up valuable pastureland and heading toward the new stables Brett had just had built.

Chapter Five

Ray jolted to a stop several hundred feet from the flames.

The fire department should be on the way, but he couldn't wait. He had to do something. He quickly scanned the blaze. One of the five barns Brett had had built was on fire, but the others were still safe, although if they didn't do something fast, it would spread.

The sound of horses whinnying and pounding their hoofs against the buildings echoed above the roar of the blaze.

He punched Brett's number, running toward the burning building to make sure it was empty as the phone rang. Three rings and his brother's voice mail kicked in. "Brett, it's Ray. There's a fire at the stables. I've called the fire department, but I need you to get over here now."

He jammed his phone into his coat pocket and checked the doorway to the first barn. Flames shot through the interior and seeped through the openings. He darted around back to the rear door and felt it. Warm, but not too hot.

He eased it open and glanced inside, heat instantly flushing his skin with perspiration. The right side of the barn was completely engulfed in flames, patches spreading through the interior, eating the floor and hay in the stalls.

No sign of horses inside, though. *Thank God.*

Still, if they didn't contain the blaze, the animals could be in danger.

He ran back outside, gulping in fresh air as he hurried to the second barn. Smoke thickened the air, the wind blowing fiery sparks into the grass by the second barn and quickly catching.

Dammit. Where was that fire engine?

Knowing he couldn't wait, he dashed inside the barn. Three horses stamped and kicked, pawing at the stalls to escape. Smoke seeped through the open doorway, making it hard to breathe.

He jogged to the first stall, unlatched the gate and yelled at the horse to get out. "Go on, buddy! It's all right."

The black gelding sprinted through the barn and outside. A siren wailed, and he ran to the next stall. The big animal was pawing and kicking wildly, obviously panicked.

"Shh, buddy, I'm going to set you free." He opened the gate, then jumped aside as the horse charged past him.

One more to go.

The siren grew louder, then the fire truck careened down the driveway and roared to a stop. Ray had reached the third stall, but the terrified horse stomped his feet. "Come on, boy, we have to get out of here."

The horse raised its front legs as he entered, whinnying and backing against the wall. Suddenly wood cracked and popped, and flames rippled along the floor in the front.

Then the scent of gasoline hit him.

Dammit to hell, had someone intentionally set the fire?

The horse jumped, his legs clawing at the air, his fear palpable.

"It's okay, boy," Ray said, forcing a calm to his voice to soothe the terrified animal. "I'm here. We have to go now."

The horse whinnied again, and Ray pulled a rope from the hook and inched his way closer, speaking softly until the horse dropped to all fours and let him approach.

He gently stroked the horse's mane, comforting him as he lifted the rope and slipped it around his neck. He slowly led him from the stall and out the back door.

Rescue workers jumped into motion shouting orders and dragging out the hoses. Brett's truck barreled up and screeched to a stop.

Ray patted the horse's back and eased the rope

from his neck. "Go, boy, get out of here!" He slapped the animal, sending him into a gallop across the pasture.

Ray swiped sweat and soot from his face as he hurried toward the firemen and his brother.

SCARLET WAS STILL shaking over the encounter with Bobby an hour later. She massaged her wrist where he'd grabbed her, knowing she'd have a bruise on it tomorrow. And not for the first time.

Bobby had resented her from the moment Joe McCullen had brought her home to live with Barbara.

She hadn't understood his reaction at the time. She'd been bounced from foster home to foster home and then she'd finally moved into the group facility, so being brought into a real family had thrilled her.

Until Bobby's resentment had festered and he'd started making her life miserable.

First it had just been ugly comments, the surly attitude at meals and school. Then the more sinister threats he'd whispered when he'd sneak up behind her in her room.

She shivered and pulled on flannel pj's as she recalled the time she'd crawled into bed and discovered a rattlesnake under the covers. Another time she'd found her bed full of spiders.

A month later, he'd tricked her into going with

him in the car one night, then he'd left her stranded in the woods alone, with no way to get home.

Worse, there was the time he'd nearly drowned her in the pond.

Each time he'd threatened to kill her if she told anyone.

And Barbara…she'd doted on Bobby. Had felt sorry for him because he'd been deprived of the McCullen name and the opportunities that had accompanied it.

Although Joe had supported Bobby and tried to bond with him, it hadn't been enough for Barbara or her son.

She'd believed everything Bobby said and justified his bad behavior with a joke about boys being boys. She'd acted as if Bobby's violent outbursts were normal teenage behavior. And she'd blamed Joe for not being around all the time.

Barbara's own resentment over the fact that Joe would never marry her had blinded her to her precious son's sadistic side.

Just as she had every night since the snake incident, Scarlet turned down the covers and examined the bed to make sure no creepy crawler was waiting for her.

She breathed out a sigh of relief that the bed was clean. But Bobby's cold look haunted her as she closed her eyes. He wouldn't be satisfied until he learned what Joe had left him.

Even then, would it be enough?

And what would happen when he finally came face-to-face with his half brothers?

RAY RAN TOWARD the third barn to check for more horses with Brett on his heels. The first barn was completely ablaze, as flames climbed the front of the second.

Wind hurled smoke and embers through the air, wood popping and crackling. The firefighters were blasting both buildings with water, working frantically to contain the blaze.

"What the hell happened?" Brett yelled as he yanked open the barn door. "How did this start?"

Sweat poured down Ray's face. "I don't know. The first barn was on fire when I arrived. I ran to the second one to save the horses."

Together they raced inside to free the terrified animals trapped in the stalls. The horses stamped and whinnied, pawing and kicking at the wooden slats. A black quarter horse protested, but Brett had a magic touch with animals and soothed him as he led him into the fresh air.

Ray eased a rope around a palomino that was balking and slowly coaxed him through the door and outside, then away from the fire.

"Go on, boy," Ray yelled as he removed the rope and patted the palomino's side. The horse broke into a run, meeting up with the other animals as they galloped across the land.

Sweat trickled down Ray's neck as he and Brett rushed inside to free the last two horses.

When they'd rescued them, he and Brett stood and watched the firefighters finish extinguishing the blaze.

"I can't believe this," Brett said, coughing at the smoke. "We just got these buildings finished and settled the horses in last week."

"The insurance was taken care of, right?"

"Yeah," Brett said with a scowl. "But this will cost us time. I was hoping to start lessons in the spring."

And time meant money. Not that Brett didn't have some from his rodeo winnings, but he had invested a good bit into building a home for him and Willow and their son.

"At least we didn't lose any horses," Brett said. "I couldn't stand to see them get hurt or suffer."

That would have been a huge financial loss, too.

Ray gritted his teeth. "I smelled gasoline, Brett."

Brett's gaze turned steely. "You mean, someone intentionally set the fire?"

"We'll have to let the arson investigator determine that, but it looks that way."

Brett reached for his phone. "We should call Maddox."

Ray shook his head. "Wait. He'll be back day after tomorrow. We can handle this until then."

Brett winced as the roof to the first barn collapsed. "You're right. He should enjoy his honeymoon."

"You said you smelled gas?" the fireman said to Ray. "I called our arson investigator. As soon as the embers cool enough for him to dig around, we'll do a thorough search."

The blaze was beginning to die down, although the first building was a total loss. The front of the second building suffered damage, but hopefully the interior and stalls had been saved.

"I should have had an automatic sprinkler system installed," Brett said glumly.

Ray detected an underlying note of blame in his brother's voice. "You couldn't have known this would happen."

The smoke thickened as the wind picked up. "Yeah, but it did."

"We'll discuss installing them in the future."

Brett gave him an odd look. "I didn't think you were going to hang around."

Ray hadn't planned to. But they still had the reading of the will and the bombshell about their father's mistress and his son to contend with.

"I'll be here for a while, at least until things get settled." Which would probably be longer than he'd first thought.

Another siren wailed, and an official fire department-issued SUV barreled down the road. A sheriff's car followed. Deputy Whitefeather had probably been notified by his 911 call.

Both vehicles careened to a stop, the deputy climbing out followed by a tall, broad-shouldered man in a uniform.

Introductions were quickly made. The arson investigator's name was Lieutenant Garret Hawk.

"What happened?" Lieutenant Hawk asked.

"When I got home, I saw smoke and found the barn on fire," Ray explained. "I called for help, then ran in to rescue the horses. That's when I smelled gasoline."

Lieutenant Hawk acknowledged the other fire-fighters with a flick of his hand. "It looks like you lost one barn and part of another."

Ray nodded. "Thanks to your men and their quick response, or it could have been so much worse."

"You think someone set the fire?" Deputy Whitefeather asked.

"Our builders certainly didn't have gasoline out here," Brett said. "But I don't know who would sabotage us this way."

Ray bit the inside of his cheek. The first person that came to mind was their half brother. If Bobby was ticked off and thought he'd been left out of the inheritance, maybe he wanted revenge.

Then again, if Bobby expected to inherit a share of the ranch, why would he want to damage any part of it? Destroying buildings would only lower the value of the property. And if he was caught, he'd face charges and go to jail.

Lieutenant Hawk moved closer to the edge of the burning embers. Ashes, soot, burned wood and leather covered the ground. He knelt and used a stick to push aside some debris. A cigarette butt lay in the pile.

"Any of you smoke?"

"Not me or Brett," Ray said.

"How about ranch hands?" Lieutenant Hawk asked.

Ray and Brett and both shrugged. "It's possible," Ray said. "But they know better than to smoke around the hay."

Deputy Whitefeather walked around the edge of the embers then went inside the second barn.

"Did your father have any enemies?" Lieutenant Hawk asked.

Brett shook his head, but Ray didn't know how to respond. He wasn't ready to divulge the truth about his father's indiscretion to a stranger, especially when Maddox and Brett were still in the dark.

He would investigate the half brother himself. If he'd tried to hurt them by setting this fire, Ray would make sure he never saw a dime of the McCullen money or any piece of the land.

Chapter Six

Scarlet jerked awake to the sound of the wind whistling through the small house. Startled, she sat up and scanned her bedroom.

Outside a tree branch banged at the window, and she shivered, still shaken by Bobby's visit. Cool air brushed her skin, causing goose bumps to skate up her arms.

Wondering why the room felt so drafty, she tiptoed to the hall, but she froze at the sight of the open doorway leading to the back deck.

She had locked that door before she'd gone to bed.

Scarlet eased back into the bedroom and retrieved her gun from her nightstand. She checked the safety, then gripped it with clammy palms as she inched to the doorway.

She paused, cocked her head to the side and listened for sounds of an intruder. The wind ruffled the papers from the file on her desk in the corner, scattering them across the floor.

She scanned the small kitchen, but everything looked in place. Everything except the open doorway.

Her house only had the one bedroom and bath, and that bath opened both to the hallway and her bedroom. No one was inside.

The only hiding place would be the coat closet. Nerves on edge, she braced herself with the gun and inched to the closet. Her hand shook as she closed her fingers around the doorknob and twisted it. Holding her breath, she pulled it open, the gun aimed.

Relief flooded her. It was empty.

A noise sounded behind her and she spun around, gun still braced, but the sound was coming from outside.

She hurried to the door and searched the woods behind the house. Dogs barked, and a figure darted through the trees, but it was so dark it was impossible to see who it was.

Had that person been inside?

Shaken, she slammed the door, then knelt to examine the lock, but the lock was intact, not broken.

She locked it again and made a mental note to buy dead bolts, even a second lock for the top of the door.

Still, tension rippled through her. Why had someone broken into her house?

Her confrontation with Bobby taunted her, and she gritted her teeth. Tormenting her with scare tactics fit his sick, twisted style.

How many times when she was a teenager had he hidden in the closet or under the bed to frighten her? Once he'd even snuck into the back of the car and hidden. When she'd gotten in to drive to the store, he'd jumped up and acted as if he was going to choke her.

Shivering at the memory, she clenched the gun to her side, went to the kitchen and made a cup of hot tea. She couldn't go back to sleep now, not with her heart still racing.

But as she passed through the room, she stooped to pick up the papers scattered on the floor.

It was a work file, one that had landed on her desk just last week. She'd been called to a domestic violence scene and had been forced to pull the two-year-old little girl, Sandy, from her home. The mother was deceased, and the father, Lloyd Pullman, had been entertaining a girlfriend. Both had been drunk and an argument had escalated into a physical altercation.

The neighbors had called to report the screams coming from next door. When she'd arrived after the police, the baby was soiled and crying, the woman bruised with a black eye. The father was in a drunken rage and in cuffs.

When she'd taken custody of the baby, he'd threatened to kill her.

She stacked the papers back in the folder with a frown. Was he out of jail now? If so, had he broken in to frighten her into giving him back his child?

THE NIGHT DRAGGED on as the firefighters finished work and watched to make sure the wind didn't reignite the fire. They had started searching the debris for evidence of foul play and had found a gasoline can a few feet from the barn, tossed into a ravine.

"He probably wore gloves, but we'll still check for prints," Lieutenant Hawk said. "Hopefully we can pull some DNA from that cigarette butt."

Ray made a mental note to find out if Bobby Lowman smoked.

"Can you think of anyone who'd want to do this?" Deputy Whitefeather asked Ray and Brett.

Brett raked a hand through his hair. "Not really. Although we might have ticked off the competition. Jebediah Holcutt started up an equine business last year. Breeds quarter horses and trains them." Brett blew out an exasperated breath. "But this is big ranch country. It can easily support two ranches offering lessons and training."

Ray considered the possibility. "True, but you're a celebrity, Brett. Given the choice between lessons from you or Jebediah, who are people going to choose?"

Brett shrugged. His brother might be a celebrity, but he was humble. He'd even talked about setting up a camp for kids with problems, a therapeutic horse camp. His wife, Willow, had actually suggested the idea because her son, Brett's little boy, had suffered trauma from being kidnapped and had blossomed under Brett's care and tutelage in the saddle.

"I can check him out for you," Deputy Whitefeather offered.

Ray and Brett exchanged a questioning look, but Brett gave a clipped nod. "Okay. Maybe we can figure this out before Maddox gets back."

"Anyone else I should look into?" the deputy asked.

"Not that I know of," Brett said. "But I haven't been in town that long. If Holcutt didn't do this, we'll talk to Maddox when he returns. He would know best if Dad had any enemies."

Ray remained silent, still contemplating Scarlet Lovett's story about their half brother. He would check out Bobby Lowman.

"What about ranch hands?" Deputy Whitefeather asked. "Anyone have a beef with your father?"

"I doubt it," Brett said. "Dad was always good to his employees."

The deputy glanced at Ray, but Ray shrugged. "Like Brett said, we haven't been back in town long."

"What about that ex-con your father just hired?" the deputy asked. "The one that was in jail for the cattle-rustling operation?"

"Gus wouldn't do this," Brett said emphatically. "If anything, he owes the McCullens for clearing his name and getting him released so he could be with his family."

"All right," Deputy Whitefeather said. "Let me know when you talk to Maddox or if you think of anyone."

A bead of sweat rolled down Ray's forehead and he removed his handkerchief from his pocket to wipe it away. But his fingers connected with the card Arlis Bennett had given him.

"Come to think of it, I ran into a man named Arlis Bennett earlier. He took over Boyle Gates's ranch and said if we were interested in selling to let him know."

Brett frowned. "Gates was the man who set up Gus Garcia."

"Maddox arrested him for his involvement in that cattle-rustling ring," Deputy Whitefeather added. "Bennett is Gates's cousin."

Ray's pulse hammered. Gates probably wanted revenge.

What if he put Bennett up to sabotaging operations at Horseshoe Creek? Maybe he even thought he could force them to sell?

SCARLET CONSIDERED CALLING the sheriff, but she had no real proof that anyone had broken in. Nothing had been moved or destroyed. The wind could have blown the file off the table instead of someone looking at it.

But she was certain she'd locked that door.

Unable to sleep, she finished her tea, then reviewed files, working on paperwork until dawn. She checked the locks again before she showered, then dressed and decided to visit The Family Farm. She'd check on Faye and the kids before heading to her office to meet with the couple adopting Corey. Connecting that little boy with a forever home was a reminder of the importance of her job.

She pulled from her drive, mindful of the speed limit since children lived in the neighborhood. Down the block, she spotted a black sedan. When she reached the street where it was parked, it pulled out behind her.

She frowned as the car rode her tail.

Irritated, she accelerated, then maneuvered a turn, hoping it would go the other direction. But it turned, as well. Hands sweating, she made a couple of more turns in an effort to lose the vehicle, but her paranoia increased as it stayed behind her.

She inhaled to calm herself. Bobby didn't drive

a black sedan. What about Lloyd Pullman? She had no idea what kind of vehicle he owned.

Her shoulders knotted with tension. She turned into the gas station, then chastised herself for being paranoid when the car finally sped by.

She sat massaging her temple for a few seconds, gathering her composure, then steered her Jeep back onto the road. Still, she checked behind her and down the street as she made the short drive to The Family Farm.

As she parked, she continued to have the eerie sense someone was watching her.

Damn Bobby for making her paranoid.

She steeled herself, determined not to allow Bobby or Lloyd Pullman to terrorize her.

The scent of coffee and maple syrup greeted her as she entered the group home, and she found Faye and Millie, the cook, in the dining room with the children who'd gathered for breakfast.

Faye looked up and smiled, and Scarlet spoke to the children, pausing to chat with each one for a few minutes.

"I dreamed about riding a pony last night," Corey told her.

She ruffled his hair. "Well, maybe that dream will come true." The couple adopting him owned a small farm.

Danny, a fourteen-year-old who'd been bounced from foster home to foster home before becoming part of the family here, scowled into his plate.

"Hey, Danny," Scarlet said softly. "I heard you aced your algebra test yesterday."

He shrugged and dug his spoon into his cereal. "Waste of time."

She ignored his sour attitude. Danny acted tough, but it was an act to cover up the fact that he was hurting.

Faye motioned for her to join her in the kitchen. Scarlet followed and poured herself a cup of coffee.

"Joe McCullen's son, Ray, stopped by here yesterday," Faye said.

Scarlet's pulse jumped. "I'm sure he wanted to know all about me. If I was legitimate."

Faye wiped her hands on her apron. "He did ask about you, and about Joe. I told him how much Joe loved this place and how he helped build the farm."

Scarlet gazed out the window at the pastures. Thankfully, the house and land were paid off, but there was very little money to build the stables and add horses like Joe had planned. No money for the garden plot and farm equipment he'd suggested so the kids could grow their own vegetables.

All the more reason she'd stand up for herself if the McCullen brothers challenged the will. She could use whatever amount Joe had left her to help around here.

"Scarlet, is something wrong?" Faye asked.

"What do you mean?"

"I never quite understood why Joe didn't tell his family about this place. Or about you."

"I didn't understand it, either," Scarlet said. "But I'm sure he had his reasons."

Still, he'd hurt Ray and Bobby.

Faye nodded, although she looked curious. But she didn't push the subject.

"I have to go, Faye. I'm supposed to meet the Fullers about Corey in an hour."

Faye's expression brightened. "Good. That boy needs a real home."

So did all the kids. But it didn't always happen.

Scarlet squeezed Faye's hand. "I know what you mean. But this is a real home, too, Faye. Thanks to you and Millie and Lois, these children have love and family."

Faye blushed, and Scarlet gave her a hug, then slipped back through the house and outside to her car. For a brief second, down the street, she thought she spotted the same car that she'd feared was following her earlier. But it disappeared around the corner. The kids were laughing and talking as they walked to the school bus stop.

She climbed in her car, chastising herself for being so nervous, then headed to her office. But on the way, she couldn't shake the sense that she was being followed again. She punched the number for the sheriff's office in Laramie.

"This is Scarlet Lovett," she said. "Is Lloyd Pullman still in custody?"

"As a matter of fact, he made bail yesterday," the deputy told her.

Scarlet inhaled sharply as his threat echoed in her head. Had Pullman broken into her house the night before? Had he been parked down the street from her and followed her this morning?

"Do you know what kind of car he drives?" Scarlet asked.

"No, why?"

The temptation to tell him her concerns nagged at her, but she didn't want him to think she was irrational. "No reason. I was just curious."

"Listen, Scarlet, if he bothers you, let me know. Or better yet, call the sheriff in Pistol Whip. He can make it to your house faster than I can."

"Thanks. I will."

She hung up, keeping her eyes alert for the sedan again. Although traffic in Pistol Whip was minimal, early morning commuters were making their way to work. She pressed the brakes to turn into her office, but her Wrangler didn't slow.

Tires squealed, and she swerved then pumped the brakes, but the vehicle sped down the small hill, gaining momentum. A pedestrian crossing the street caught her eye, and she pounded the horn, terrified she was going to hit the woman. The woman screamed and darted to the sidewalk, just as Scarlet jerked the steering wheel to the right.

The Wrangler careened forward, tires bumping over the sidewalk. She was losing control and struggled to keep from crashing into the hair salon, but as she veered to the right to avoid it, she flew toward her own office building.

Seconds later, she screamed, glass pelting her from the windshield as the Wrangler rammed into the brick wall.

Chapter Seven

Glass shattered and pelted Scarlet, and her head snapped back as the air bag deployed.

Her lungs felt as if they exploded as the impact threw her forward.

She blinked, slightly dizzy from the force of the crash. What had just happened?

Her brakes…they hadn't worked…

Suddenly a shout erupted outside the vehicle. "Scarlet!"

Someone jerked at the driver's door. Reality fought through the shock immobilizing her, and she pushed at the air bag, searching for her seat belt. Her fingers found the hook, but when she tried to unfasten it, it was stuck. For a moment, panic seized her. She couldn't breathe. Her head hurt. Her legs felt numb.

Dear God…she couldn't move them.

Then the door swung open, and she heard the voice again. "Scarlet, are you all right?"

Her assistant, Hugh Weatherman. He must have had a pocketknife, because a second later, he ripped away the air bag and freed her. She was trembling all over as he cut away the seat belt.

"I called 911 when I heard the crash," Hugh said. "Are you hurt?"

It took another minute for Scarlet to pull herself from the shock. "I don't know." She tried to move her legs, but her right one was stuck.

"Stay still," Hugh said. "The medics are on the way."

She nodded, numb and terrified.

Hugh pulled out a handkerchief and wiped at her cheek. "You're bleeding. Are you in pain?"

She shook her head. "No, but I can't move my legs."

"The front end is crunched," Hugh said. "You're probably just trapped by the metal."

A tremor rippled through her, and she fought back a cry of panic.

"Just hang in there, Scarlet, we'll get you out."

A siren wailed, lights flashing, and Scarlet laid her head back against the seat and tried to stay calm. A minute later, tires screeched as an ambulance and fire truck roared to stops.

Hugh yelled and waved them over, and a female medic greeted her. "You all right, ma'am?"

She nodded. "I think so. But my legs are trapped."

A fireman appeared behind her to assess the

situation, and Scarlet braced herself as they began the process of sawing away the metal to free her.

RAY LET HIMSELF sleep for a couple of hours, but then hurriedly showered, dressed and headed to the deputy sheriff's office. Brett had already called the insurance company to handle the claim. He also insisted that they'd rebuild immediately.

But they had to find out who set the fire and prevent more sabotage.

Ray wanted answers and he wanted them before Maddox returned.

He entered the sheriff's office and found Deputy Whitefeather on the phone.

"Yes. I'll be right there." He hung up and grabbed his jacket. "Sorry, McCullen, there's been an accident. I need to go."

Dammit, Ray wanted to ask for his help looking into Bobby Lowman. "What happened?"

"Lady named Scarlet Lovett crashed her Jeep into the side of the building where she works. They're cutting her out of it."

Ray's heart hammered. "Is she all right?"

"I don't know. The ambulance is there now." He strode to the door, his keys jangling in his hand.

"I'll follow you," Ray said.

The deputy's brows furrowed. "Why? Do you know her?"

Ray gave a clipped nod. "Not well, but we've met."

"Suit yourself." Deputy Whitefeather hurried outside, and Ray jogged to his SUV and followed him.

More gray skies hid the sun, making the air feel chillier than it was. Wind beat at the trees, whipping tumbleweed across the side of the road as they turned onto a side street.

A stand-alone brick building bearing a sign for Social Services stood between the library and an empty warehouse.

The deputy veered into the parking lot, and Ray followed, his breath tightening at the sight of the Wrangler crunched into the brick structure. Just as he parked, the rescue workers pulled away a chunk of metal.

He parked and climbed out, tensing at the sight of the medics working to extract Scarlet.

In spite of the chill, sweat rolled down the back of his neck. Had she been hurt?

The deputy greeted one of the rescue workers and gestured toward the Wrangler. "What happened?"

"She said the brakes failed," the worker said. "She tried to stop but couldn't."

Ray's instincts jumped to life. The fact that Scarlet had just visited him and told him about her relationship to Joe and the will, then the ranch had been sabotaged and now she'd had an accident, all struck him as odd.

And too coincidental.

Had her car crash really been an accident?

A female medic was leaning over Scarlet checking her blood pressure. From his vantage point, he couldn't see if she was seriously injured.

He made his way to the stretcher just as the medics started to load her into the ambulance. "Scarlet?"

She groaned, and Ray's chest tightened. Blood dotted her arms and her cheeks looked pale, also speckled with blood. The medics had secured her neck and body on the board with straps, so she couldn't turn her head.

He stepped up beside her so she could see his face, but the deputy edged his way beside him and spoke first. "What happened?" Deputy Whitefeather asked.

"I don't know," she said in a raspy whisper. "I was on my way to the office when the brakes failed."

Ray gritted his teeth as the medic frowned at him. "We need to get her to the hospital," the female said. "She needs tests to make sure she didn't sustain internal injuries."

"Ray?" Scarlet said in a low voice.

He squeezed her hand, feeling the tremor running through her. He couldn't blame her for being shaken. She could have been killed. "I'll meet you at the hospital, Scarlet."

The deputy gave him a questioning look, but Ray ignored it. The medics loaded her in the back of the ambulance, then the driver circled to the front, hopped in and they sped off.

"How do you know her?" Deputy Whitefeather asked.

"She was close to my father," Ray said, giving away as little information as possible. He went to examine the Wrangler while the rescue workers stowed their equipment.

When Ray had first left the ranch, he'd worked at a garage. He wanted a look at those brake lines.

The deputy stepped up beside him. "What's going on, McCullen?"

"I don't know," Ray said as he examined the car. "It looks as if her brake lines were cut."

A frown marred the tall Native American's face. "First a fire is set at your ranch, now someone cut this woman's brakes." He lifted his hat and scratched his head. "What aren't you telling me? Do you think these incidences are connected?"

Maybe. Although if Jebediah Holcutt or Arlis Bennett had set the fire at the ranch, they wouldn't have any reason to hurt Scarlet.

But Bobby Lowman had motive to do both. Still, Ray couldn't divulge family secrets to this stranger, not before he had a chance to talk to Maddox and Brett.

"I don't know. It'd be best to talk to Scarlet and see who might want to hurt her."

SCARLET WAS SO relieved that she could move her legs and that she had no serious injuries that she wanted to shout. How could she have helped the kids at the orphanage if she'd been paralyzed or injured and needed a long recovery time?

But as the staff finished running tests and cleaned the small cuts and abrasions she'd received from the shattered glass, she replayed the morning in her head.

Her car had worked fine on the way to the orphanage, but she'd thought someone was following her. She also thought she'd seen the same car near The Family Farm. Had the driver cut her brakes while she was inside with the children?

The doctor shined a light in her eyes. "Did you hit your head?"

She blinked and followed the light as he moved it from side to side. "No. The air bag and seat belt saved me."

"Good thing. Although we probably should keep you overnight for observation."

"That's not necessary," Scarlet said. "I'm a little sore, but I'm okay."

He studied her for another moment. "All right. But if you feel dizzy or nauseous, come back. You may have a slight concussion."

Scarlet quickly agreed. Hospitals reminded her of being sick when she was young. Of needles and white coats and sterile odors and...being scared and alone.

She wanted to go home.

The doctor paused at the doorway. "Deputy Whitefeather is outside waiting to talk to you."

She nodded, smoothing out her tangled hair as a nurse escorted the deputy into the room. To her surprise, Ray McCullen followed him inside.

"The doctor said you don't have any serious injuries?" Ray asked.

"Yes. I guess I was lucky." Especially considering the way her car was crunched. "My ribs are bruised and I'm banged up, but I'm fine."

Ray's look darkened. "I wouldn't exactly say you were lucky."

"He's right," Deputy Whitefeather said. "Ray examined your car and so did a mechanic. Your brake lines were cut."

Scarlet's breath rushed out. "You mean someone intentionally wanted them to fail?"

"Yes," Ray said through clenched teeth.

Scarlet's heart hammered with fear. "I...I can't believe this."

"Miss Lovett," Deputy Whitefeather said. "Can you think of anyone who would want to hurt you?"

Scarlet glanced at Ray, her stomach churning. Bobby was at the top of the list. "I've made a few enemies with my job," Scarlet said, hesitant to point the finger at anyone.

"Someone specific come to mind?"

She ran a finger over the bandage on her arm. "A man named Lloyd Pullman was arrested for abuse. I removed his daughter from his custody. He was irate and threatened me."

Deputy Whitefeather tugged a small notebook from his pocket and clicked his pen, then jotted down the information. "Where is he?"

"I don't know." Scarlet wet her lips. Her mouth was so dry she felt as if she couldn't swallow. "Apparently Pullman made bail yesterday."

"I'll issue a BOLO for him and bring him in for questioning."

The deputy stepped from the room with his phone, and Ray moved closer. He paused at the edge of the bed then lifted a finger to trace the bandage on her forehead. "Does it hurt?" Ray asked.

She shrugged, her skin tingling at the concern in his voice. "Not much. I'm tough, Ray. I'll be all right."

"That's not the point," he said in a gruff tone. "The point is that someone tried to kill you."

His words sucked the air from her lungs again. Pullman had reason to hurt her. And Bobby despised her.

But Ray had reason to dislike her, too. If she was gone, she couldn't demand the McCullens make good on Joe's will.

Although she couldn't imagine Ray hurting a woman.

He lifted her arm and rubbed a finger over the

bruise on her wrist. "You didn't get this from the accident, did you?"

Shame washed over her. On a conscious level, she knew that when a man abused a woman, it was not the woman's fault. But she also understood the vulnerability the victim felt.

She had decided long ago not to be a victim.

Bobby had caught her off guard last night. She wouldn't let it happen again.

RAY SILENTLY WILLED his temper in check. The moment he'd seen that bruise on Scarlet's wrist he'd known it wasn't caused by the accident. Hell, he could easily see a man's thumbprint where he'd gripped her.

"How did this happen? Was it Bobby?"

She bit her lip and nodded. "He came by last night. He was…upset."

"That doesn't mean he has the right to hurt you."

"I know that." Scarlet stiffened, then slid her legs over the side of the bed. "I handled the situation, Ray."

"How did you handle it?" he asked. "Did you call the deputy?"

Her hair fell over the side of her face like a curtain of gold as she shook her head. "I stopped him," she said. "Trust me, Ray. I'm not the kind of girl who allows a guy to beat up on her. I learned that lesson a long time ago."

Her words both infuriated him and stirred admiration for her. She might look like one of those porcelain dolls his mother had collected, but she was tough as nails and had spunk.

Her legs buckled as she attempted to stand, though, and she muttered a sound of frustration as she reached for the bed to steady herself. "I don't have time for this. I had a meeting today."

Ray placed his hands on top of hers, lowering his tone to a soothing pitch. "Don't worry about your appointments. Your assistant, Hugh, said he would reschedule."

She gave him a determined look. "That meeting is important, Ray. A family wants to adopt one of the little boys at The Family Farm. Corey is counting on me."

"I'm sure it'll work out," Ray said. "Now, I'm going to drive you home so you can rest."

Her gaze met his, a myriad of emotions glittering in her eyes. She didn't like being vulnerable or in debt to anyone, he could see that.

But she was in danger, and quite possibly from her own adopted brother who was irate because of their father.

He made a split-second decision. Deputy Whitefeather would investigate Pullman.

Ray would personally look into Bobby. Hell, he'd planned to anyway.

And if he'd tried to kill Scarlet, blood kin or not, the bastard would regret it.

Chapter Eight

Scarlet winced as she climbed in the passenger seat of Ray's Range Rover. "I could have called someone else, Ray. You don't have to drive me home."

Ray's jaw tightened. "It's not a problem, Scarlet. We need to talk anyway."

Talk? Had he told his brothers about her and Bobby? Had he already found a loophole to exclude them from their inheritance?

She rubbed her forehead and waited, not sure she wanted the answer. She'd fight for her share for the children at the home.

But she was tired right now, her head ached and she needed to pull herself together.

"Where is your place?" Ray asked.

She gave him directions, anxious as he made the turn onto the street where she lived. The houses were small but well kept. The children's toys in the yards indicated it was a family neighborhood. That was one reason she'd chosen it. She liked the homey feel.

"The one at the end," Scarlet said.

Ray pulled into the drive, but made no comment. He seemed to be assessing the place, though, as they walked up the path to the house.

"Can I come in?" he asked when she unlocked the door.

She supposed she might as well get it over with. "Sure." She went inside and dropped her purse on the table by the door, then walked to the kitchen.

"Coffee?"

"Don't go to any trouble for me."

"I'm not, I need a cup," Scarlet said. "It's been a long morning."

She made quick work of brewing a pot while he simply stood and watched her, his silence as unnerving as the dark intensity in his brown eyes.

When she handed him a mug, their fingers brushed and a tingle traveled up her spine. Her gaze flew to his, and something sparked in his eyes as if he'd felt it, too.

Dear heavens, was she so shaken and lonely that she was imagining a connection between the two of them? An attraction?

Ray probably saw her as an enemy or a problem he needed to get rid of.

Ray cleared his throat. "What exactly happened today?"

Scarlet carried her coffee to the den, turned

on the gas logs and sank onto the couch. Ray followed, but stood by the fireplace, his posture rigid.

"I went to The Family Farm to check on things. Then I was on my way to the office to meet with this couple about an adoption."

"Anything unusual about that? Any problems with the adoption?"

She frowned as she replayed the morning in her head. "Not with the adoption. Corey's parents died in a car accident and he has no family. So there was no one contesting the adoption, if that's what you mean."

Ray gave a small nod. "Your car was running okay on the way there?"

A shaky sigh escaped her. "Yes. Although...I thought someone was following me when I first left home." She picked at a thread on the afghan. "It was a black sedan. I noticed it down the street when I left and it pulled out behind me."

Ray's brows arched. "Did you see the driver?"

"No." She dragged the afghan onto her lap. "Although my nerves were on edge because last night I woke up and the door to the outside was open. I locked it before I went to bed, so I was afraid someone was inside."

Ray's expression hardened. "Did you report the break-in?"

She shook her head. "I searched the house, but there was nobody inside. Nothing was disturbed or taken. I figured the police would just think I left the door unlocked, and that the wind blew it open."

Ray made a low sound in his throat. "So you had a break-in, then you thought someone was following you this morning?"

"Yes. The sedan stayed behind me for a while. I turned into a gas station to see if it followed, then the car went on."

"You know anyone who drives a car like that?"

She sipped her coffee. "No, not that I can think of."

"What about Pullman?"

"I don't know what he drives."

"But he's dangerous?"

She nodded and sipped her coffee. "He was furious that I put his daughter into foster care. But I had no choice."

"You said he threatened you?"

"He did," Scarlet said. "I told him the court would require him to attend counseling if he wanted to be reunited with her. His wife's parents are supposed to be flying in soon and are asking for custody."

Ray glanced into the fire, then back at her and her arm where the bruise had turned a dark purple. "When did you see Bobby?"

"He came by last night." Scarlet relayed their conversation in her head. "I told him about our talk. He was furious that Joe included me in the will."

"Then he grabbed you?"

"Yes," she said, determined not to reveal how much Bobby frightened her. "But I informed him that Joe also included him, and that appeased him slightly."

"So he left peacefully?"

"Not exactly. I pulled my gun on him and ordered him to leave. Bobby doesn't like to be shown up, especially by a woman."

"So he could have come back and broken in to scare you? And he could have followed you and cut your brake lines?"

"I guess it's possible."

Ray cleared his throat then sat down beside her. When his hand touched her arm again, that same ripple of awareness shot through her.

"My brother Brett started building stables for the horses where he plans to expand the ranch operations."

She frowned, confused.

"Someone set fire to them last night, Scarlet."

Scarlet's pulse clamored as the implications of his statement set in. Bobby had been upset with her and left in a rage. And he hated the McCullens.

Had he set fire to the barns to get back at Ray and his brothers?

RAY STUDIED SCARLET, disturbed by the feelings she aroused. He should have been suspicious of her. But his father had included her in his will and had cared for her.

He was beginning to understand the reason. She helped needy children and fought for what was right.

He didn't think she was capable of hurting anyone or causing damage to someone's property, especially with a fire. He saw no signs of ashtrays or cigarettes in her house either, and didn't peg her as a smoker.

Bobby, on the other hand, might not feel he was receiving enough compensation for being Joe's son.

He hated to admit it, but Bobby had reason to hate him and his brothers.

Scarlet hugged the blanket to her with a sigh.

Ray fought the urge to pull her in his arms. "I can see the wheels turning in your head, Scarlet. What are you thinking?"

Scarlet traced a finger around the rim of her coffee mug. "I don't know what to think," she said, her voice soft. Pained. "I hate to think that Lloyd Pullman would try to kill me. And I hate even more to think that Bobby set that fire at the ranch. But I know Bobby." She rubbed her wrist in a self-conscious gesture.

Ray arched a brow. "You think he's capable?"

Scarlet leaned her head back against the sofa,

making Ray feel guilty. She probably had a killer of a headache and needed to lie down. "I'm sorry, if you need to rest, I'll go."

She shook her head. "No, we might as well talk about the situation. If Bobby is responsible for that fire or my accident, it's best we face it."

Her directness made his respect for her grow. Dammit, he didn't want to like her, but he did. No wonder his father had…helped her.

"Bobby smokes, and he likes fire. He used to burn trash in the backyard all the time. A couple of times when we were teenagers some of my things went missing. I saw him set them on fire outside in a garbage can."

Ray hissed between his teeth. "Go on."

"I was ten when Joe first introduced me to Barbara. Bobby was fourteen. He had just hit puberty and was brooding and sullen."

Ray had been angry himself at that age. Angry because his father had cheated on his mother. And because his mother was gone. Killed by a drunk driver. But he hadn't set fire to things.

"Were my father and Barbara still involved then?"

Her eyes flickered with uncertainty. "Are you sure you want to hear this?"

"My mother was dead by then, Scarlet. I'm surprised he didn't marry Barbara after that."

"I think the guilt ate at him," Scarlet said. "Joe

once told me your mother was the only woman he ever loved."

Emotions crowded Ray's chest, but he cleared his throat, determined not to let them show. Anger had been his best friend for so long that he didn't know what he'd do without it. It kept him strong.

"Then why did he keep seeing Barbara?"

Scarlet shrugged. "Barbara was in love with Joe," Scarlet said. "She could be charming and hard to resist. I think she met Joe in a weak moment, maybe when he and your mother were having some trouble, and he slept with her. When she gave birth to Bobby, he felt tied to her."

"But he kept coming back," Ray said, his voice hard.

"I can't explain, Ray. I don't understand myself. There was something there. Joe cared about Barbara. After all, she had his child. And he couldn't just desert her."

But he couldn't bring her into his family, either. He'd kept them separate, a secret from Maddox and Brett.

God, Ray dreaded telling them. Had hoped he'd at least understand the problem more when he did.

"Did Barbara pressure Dad to marry her?"

Scarlet massaged her temple. "Maybe before I came along. As I grew older, I realized that she took me in to please Joe. That she thought he might marry her if she did."

"But then he didn't marry her," Ray said. "Did she resent you for that?"

Scarlet closed her eyes on a sigh. "Some, I think. Honestly, I'd been shuffled through so many foster homes before I wound up in the group home that I was simply glad to have a home without an abusive man in it."

Ray gripped his coffee cup so hard he thought he might break it. He didn't know if he wanted to hear the rest of her story, at least not that part.

"But then Bobby turned out to be just as bad."

He sat up straighter. "What do you mean?"

"He used to taunt me when no one was around. Play mean tricks on me. Put snakes in my bed. Lock me in the closet." She hesitated. "His animosity escalated when he started drinking, and he got rough."

He sucked in a breath. "How rough?"

"He knocked me around a few times, but usually the bruises weren't visible."

"What about Barbara? Didn't she do anything?"

Scarlet made a sarcastic sound in her throat. "She didn't know. As far as she was concerned, Bobby hung the moon. He was like a chameleon—he could put on an act when she was around that made him look like a saint."

Ray gripped his hands by his sides. Damn, he was beginning to detest his half brother.

"Did my father spend time with Bobby?"

"He tried," Scarlet said. "But Bobby was difficult. He was always getting in trouble, and he was belligerent with Joe."

So he and Bobby had both given his father hell.

"Did he get in trouble with the law?"

Scarlet nodded. "I think Joe paid someone to seal his juvenile record."

"What was he arrested for?"

"Vandalism, carrying a weapon to school, breaking and entering, DUI."

"Good grief," Ray muttered.

She fiddled with her hair. "I think he pulled a knife on a guy in a bar one night, too."

Ray contemplated all she'd said. "You said Bobby smokes and that he likes to burn things?"

She touched her leg and absentmindedly rubbed the top of her thigh, drawing his attention there. And making him wonder what had happened.

"Yes."

Had he burned her with a cigarette?

His mind took a leap. "Scarlet?"

Scarlet looked up at him, her face pale. "The vandalism charge—he and some of his buddies set fire to an old warehouse just to watch it burn."

Chapter Nine

If Ray had any doubt about the validity of Scarlet's story and the fact that Joe had cared for her, the photograph in the frame on the mantel alleviated it. In the picture, Joe stood beside a knobby-kneed teenage girl with pigtails and freckles. She sat in the saddle of a beautiful palomino, her eyes lit with joy while his father looked…softer than he'd ever seen him.

Another photograph showed his father, Scarlet and a brunette woman he assumed to be Barbara around a table holding a birthday cake with Scarlet's name on it. Scarlet looked to be about sixteen and was blowing out the candles, while the skinny, tall boy next to her glared at her. The boy had to be Bobby.

Ray tried to see a resemblance between Joe and Bobby, but didn't.

"I think it's time I met Bobby." Ray stood and

glanced around the small living room. "Do you feel safe here?"

Scarlet pushed a strand of that silky hair from her forehead. "Yes. I have my gun." She reached for her purse and retrieved her cell phone. "I'm going to call about getting new locks installed, too."

"Good idea. Where does Bobby live?"

Scarlet winced as she shifted on the sofa. "I don't know. I haven't seen him in months. He just showed up out of the blue."

"Would Barbara know?"

Scarlet nodded. "Probably. But if you're going to talk to her, let's go together. She can be a charmer, but I can usually tell when she's lying."

Ray considered her suggestion. "Confronting Barbara might be dangerous, especially if she's aware her son is causing trouble."

"If she knows, she'll protect him," Scarlet said. "That's why I want to go. I need to see her reaction when she hears about my accident and the fire."

Ray's phone buzzed, and he checked the number. Brett. "It's my brother. Let me take this."

He punched Connect then walked over to the window and studied the woods behind Scarlet's house.

"I've talked with the insurance company and the arson investigator is taking care of his end of the deal," Brett said. "The deputy said Jebediah Holcutt has been out of town for two weeks on a buying trip. So he's not our guy." Brett sighed. "I also asked the foreman to have the ranch hands meet me in the dining hall."

"What time?"

"Half an hour."

"I'll meet you there."

"You sure?"

"Yeah. Someone attacks Horseshoe Creek, the McCullen men have to stick together."

Brett agreed, and Ray hung up and turned back to Scarlet. "Get those locks changed while I meet with my brother and the ranch hands. Then I'll come back and we'll pay Barbara a visit."

It was high time he met his father's mistress. He wanted to know if she had her own agenda before he dropped the bombshell about her and Bobby in his brothers' laps.

SCARLET CALLED A locksmith as soon as Ray left, then the mechanic who'd helped The Family Farm find an inexpensive van to transport the children to activities. He also fixed up used cars and sold them, and agreed to drop off a rental car for her.

Then she phoned Faye to explain what had happened while she waited for the locksmith to arrive.

"Are you sure you're okay?" Faye asked.

"Yes, I'm fine. Just let the kids know I'll be back as soon as possible."

Faye agreed and she ended the call and phoned Hugh. He'd already left a message on her cell.

"I'm really okay," she assured him. "Did you meet the Fullers?"

"Yes, and they finished the paperwork. I sent it on through, so hopefully things will progress quickly."

"You're a lifesaver, Hugh. I don't know what I'd do without you."

"Ahh, I feel the same way, Scarlet. You know I'd do anything for you."

Scarlet hesitated before responding. Lately she'd sensed Hugh had a crush on her and didn't want to lead him on. But she didn't feel that spark when she looked at him.

Not like she felt with Ray.

But she couldn't allow herself to be attracted to Joe's son. For heaven's sake, if she acted as if she wanted a romantic relationship with him, he'd probably think she was after a bigger share of Horseshoe Creek.

The doorbell dinged, and she stood, grateful for the intrusion. "Thanks, Hugh. I have to go. I called a locksmith. He's here now."

"Okay. Do you want me to come by and stay with you later? I can bring dinner."

"I appreciate it, Hugh, but I'm going to visit Barbara."

"All right. But call me if you need me."

She thanked him, disconnected and rushed to answer the door.

A chuffy balding man in a gray uniform bearing the logo of the security company stood on the stoop with a clipboard. "Miss Lovett?"

"Yes." She motioned for him to come in.

"What exactly do you want done here?"

"I need dead bolts on all the doors along with a top lock on the French doors off the patio."

"Are you interested in a security system?"

"I would like one, but this is a rental house." Maybe she would ask the owner to install one. Although he'd probably up the rent and she could barely cover her bills on her salary now.

She stepped into the kitchen while he retrieved tools and supplies from his work van. While he worked on the locks, she punched Barbara's number. She worked at a hair salon in Laramie named Sassy's, but she'd always hoped that Joe would marry her and she could quit.

Barbara finally answered on the fifth ring. "Hello."

"It's Scarlet, Barbara. I need to see you."

A long-winded, exasperated sigh. "What about?"

"Joe and his will."

Tension stretched between them for a full second before Barbara finally replied. "Fine. Meet me at the house in a couple of hours."

"I will." Scarlet said goodbye without mentioning that she would be bringing Joe's son with her.

She wanted to see Barbara's gut reaction when Ray showed up on her doorstep.

BRETT WAS ALREADY inside the dining hall when Ray arrived. He parked outside, noting two ranch hands smoking beside the back porch. His suspicious nature kicked in, but he reminded himself that it wasn't uncommon for cowboys in Wyoming to either smoke or chew tobacco.

They would have to wait until the lab analyzed DNA on the cigarette butt found at the fire to determine who had dropped it in the barn.

The low rumbling of voices echoed through the front door as he entered. The place smelled like barbecue and cherry pie. Judging from the empty plates in front of the workers at the long wooden table, dinner must have been pretty damn good.

Ray had yet to meet everyone, and heads turned as he walked past the table to join Brett.

Brett clanged a big metal spoon against one of the pots to get the men's attention.

"I appreciate you all showing up," Brett said.

Clyde Hammerstone, the head foreman waved his hand in the air. "We're missing five guys. They're moving the herd from the east pasture to the south today."

Brett nodded. "I'll talk to them when they get back. But I wanted to tell you all what happened last night."

"You had a fire, didn't you?" a young guy in a

cowboy hat and red shirt asked. "I heard the siren and saw smoke."

Brett explained about losing the barn and the damage to the other one. "If we hadn't arrived when we did, we might have lost the horses."

Concerned murmurs rumbled through the room.

"What caused it?" another ranch hand asked.

"That's the problem," Brett said. "We found a cigarette butt in the barn and smelled gasoline."

The two men Ray had seen smoking stepped inside the side door, but hung back. One was big and hairy with a scar over his right eye. The other man was thinner and walked with a limp.

Clyde coughed, a shocked look in his eyes. "You think someone set that fire on purpose?"

The young man in the hat and red shirt shot up from his seat. "Is that why you called us together? You think one of us did it?"

Brett and Ray exchanged a worried look, and Ray stepped up to speak. "I'm Ray, the youngest of Joe's sons. We're not accusing you of anything. Our father hired people he could trust and hand-picked each one of you."

"Damn right he did," Clyde stammered.

"We respected your daddy," an older man with a salt-and-pepper beard said. "I worked for him fifteen years. I'd never do anything to dishonor him."

Ray cleared his throat. "That's the reason we

called you here. We want your help. If you've seen anyone or anything suspicious around the ranch lately, let us know."

"Could be a strange vehicle or someone sneaking around," Brett interjected. "Or maybe you know someone who wants to sabotage this horse operation."

Disgruntled looks and words echoed through the room, and the two men Ray had seen smoking outside, spoke in a hushed tone to each other.

"I'm offering a ten-thousand-dollar reward for information that leads to the culprit's arrest," Brett added.

The men shifted and muttered, charging the atmosphere with tension.

If someone on the ranch knew anything helpful, that reward might tip them into talking.

The men began to disperse, talking low among themselves, and the two smokers inched toward the back door.

Ray gestured toward them. "Brett, do you know who those guys are?"

Brett narrowed his eyes to study them. "No, why?"

"I saw them smoking outside."

"A lot of the guys smoke," Brett said.

"I know." Ray chewed the inside of his cheek. "But they looked nervous."

"I'll check the work files and see what I can find on them."

"Thanks." Ray added them to the possible list of suspects. But first he had to talk to his father's mistress.

SCARLET HAD BEEN anxious about meeting the McCullen brothers, but being with Ray the first time he met Barbara compounded her nerves.

"Did you have the locks installed?" Ray asked as he opened the passenger door to his Range Rover for her.

"Yes. Hopefully the house is more secure now."

He closed the door and went around to the driver's side while she fastened her seat belt.

"I called Barbara at work and we're meeting at her house," she said. "But I didn't mention that you'd be with me."

"Good."

"Did you find out who set the fire?"

"Not yet." Ray started the engine and pulled from her driveway. She gave him Barbara's address and he entered it in his GPS, then drove toward Laramie. "Brett called the ranch hands together and offered a reward for anyone with information."

"Money usually talks," Scarlet said under her breath.

"We'll see."

Scarlet tried to ease the tension. "I was surprised to hear that he was giving up the rodeo."

Ray shrugged. "Me, too. But I think he'd had

enough of the publicity. Besides, he always had a thing for Willow James, and when he learned they had a child, he wanted to be with them." He cast her a questioning look. "Did my father talk about Willow and Sam? Did he know Sam was Brett's?"

Scarlet shifted, uncomfortable with the question. Joe had shared some of his feelings about the distance between his sons, but those had been private, heartfelt confessions. "He didn't say anything specific about the little boy. But he definitely missed you and Brett and wanted you to come home."

Ray fell silent and clenched his jaw as he drove, and Scarlet decided not to push the subject. They all had emotional baggage and were grieving. Only time and forgiveness would heal the wounds.

The rest of the ride passed in silence.

Scarlet hadn't visited Barbara in months and was surprised to see that she'd let the yard get overgrown. The shutters on the house needed painting and the bushes trimming.

Ray parked and turned to her. "Barbara probably hated us, didn't she? She blamed us for keeping our father from her."

"Ray, I can't begin to explain their complicated relationship."

"Was she prone to violence like her son? Did she ever hit you?"

Scarlet's face flushed with heat. She was torn between reality and gratitude for what Barbara had given her. Yet at the same time, Barbara's dysfunctional relationship with Bobby and with Joe had been difficult, especially since she was caught in the middle.

And according to Bobby, an outsider.

"Scarlet?"

"No, she never hit me. She was actually nice to me at first. But as Bobby became more troubled, she had to give allegiance to her *real* child." She clutched the door handle. "I became part of the problem, another person who agitated Bobby and took time from Joe that he should have given her son." She sighed and opened the car door. "When I turned eighteen, I moved out on my own."

Ray's eyes darkened with questions. "How did you manage? Did my father help you?"

Was that derision in his voice?

"No, Ray. He offered, but I worked after school and summers waitressing and saved enough money to rent a room in an older house. I landed a scholarship and eventually earned my degree in social work."

Ray cleared his throat. "I'm sure Dad was proud of you."

"He was proud of you and your brothers, too, Ray." Scarlet touched his hand, aware again that her body tingled at the touch.

A sea of emotions clouded Ray's eyes, but the front door opened and Barbara appeared. Scarlet dropped Ray's hand, and she and Ray walked up the sidewalk together.

"Hello, Barbara," Scarlet said. "This is Ray McCullen. He wanted to meet you."

"Oh, my goodness," Barbara said with a slightly false ring to her voice. "This is a surprise. Scarlet should have told me you were coming."

"I know it's sudden, but I figured it was time we met." Ray shook her hand.

"Yes, I suppose so," she said as she released his hand. Then Barbara pulled Scarlet to her for a hug.

Scarlet stiffened, unaccustomed to her affection.

The moment didn't last long, either. Barbara whispered in her ear so only she could hear, "You're more devious than I gave you credit for, Scarlet. Now that Joe is dead, you're cozying up to his son to see what else you can weasel out of the McCullens."

Pain knifed through Scarlet at Barbara's accusation. Did Barbara really think she would sleep with Ray for money?

Chapter Ten

Ray didn't know what to expect from Barbara, but at least she hadn't shut the door in his face. Scarlet's earlier comment about Barbara's fake charm made him instantly wary.

Judging from Scarlet's pained expression, the woman must have said something hurtful when they'd hugged.

Scarlet straightened and pulled away from Barbara, her look chilly. "Ray and I just met," she said flatly.

Barbara invited them in and offered coffee, but they both declined. While he and Scarlet followed the woman to her den, he studied her, searching for whatever had drawn his father to her.

Barbara was probably in her late forties, attractive with wavy brown hair. Her voice dripped with honey, as if she was from the Deep South.

Her house was modest with simple furnishings, although she definitely liked frills and had decorated with yellow, orange and bright green, versus the earthy tones of the ranch. Of course, his father had lived with three sons, so the feminine touch had been missing in their home for years.

This house was in a neighborhood as well, no sprawling ranch with stables or barns or livestock, although he had noticed a gardening shed in the back. Had Barbara been content here or had she wanted a big place like Horseshoe Creek?

"I wondered when we would meet," Barbara said. "I expected that your father would introduce us at some point, but I guess he never felt comfortable doing that." Resentment laced her voice. "You're the youngest, right?"

Ray nodded.

"You knew about me?"

"Yes. When I was young, I saw the two of you together."

Barbara tapped a cigarette from a pack on the table and rolled it between her fingers. Ray remembered the cigarette butt they'd found at the fire. Was this one the same brand?

"I never meant to hurt your family and neither did your father. But he was going through a tough time back then and...well, I'm not going to make excuses. It...we just happened. I fell in love with Joe."

She held the cigarette up and looked at it for a moment, then tossed it on the table. "I'm trying to quit."

"How's that working?" Scarlet asked.

"Easier to give up than it was to give up Joe."

Ray waited, hoping she'd elaborate. But as he scanned the room, he saw a photograph of his father with Barbara, Bobby and Scarlet on the mantel, and betrayal burned his gut. It was sobering to see the truth—that his father had two different families and that he loved both of them.

But in loving them, he'd hurt everyone involved.

"Joe loved your mother, Ray," Barbara said, drawing him back to the conversation. "Funny, but I even admired him for that loyalty. I guess that's why I hung in there. I kept thinking that one day he'd love me enough to bring me home to Horseshoe Creek. That he'd be that loyal to me."

"If he'd been that loyal, he wouldn't have cheated," Ray said.

Barbara's look softened. "It's more complicated than that, Ray."

"I thought you weren't going to make excuses." He couldn't help the bitterness in his voice.

And despite Barbara's declaration of love, his father hadn't brought her back to the ranch or made her his wife. She must have resented that.

Barbara toyed with her bangs, pushing them aside. "I'm not. Joe knew he'd disappointed you when you found out about the affair. He never forgave himself for that."

Yet he hadn't totally given up Barbara, either.

"His guilt is the reason he couldn't bear to bring me and my son to the ranch."

That made sense. "That's one reason I'm here. About your son."

She angled her head, her eyes probing him. "You know about Bobby?"

Ray nodded. "Yes, Scarlet told me."

Disapproval glinted in her eyes as she looked at Scarlet. "I suppose you explained how you came to live with me."

"Yes," Scarlet said. "I told him about Joe volunteering at the children's home."

"He was devoted to that place," Barbara said, a note of fondness in her voice. "Apparently, when he was growing up, his best friend was in foster care. When he learned about the home near Pistol Whip, he dropped by to see what it was like. Then he decided to help make it a better place." She twined her hands together. "He got attached to Scarlet and brought her home."

"But your son wasn't too happy about that, was he?" Ray asked.

Barbara's smile faded. "He was an adolescent. Bobby needed more of Joe, not to share him…"

The sentence trailed off, and Ray filled in the blanks. He didn't want to share him with someone who wasn't even a McCullen.

Ray cleared his throat. "I'd like to meet Bobby."

"Really?"

"Yes, I figured we should introduce ourselves before the reading of the will."

She narrowed her eyes. "What's really going on, Ray? Scarlet? I know you're not here to suggest we all get together and be one happy family."

No, that wasn't in the plans, Ray thought. But if he explained about the fire, she'd know he suspected her son of arson and she'd warn him.

Then Bobby might run.

THE FRONT DOOR swung open, and Bobby loped in. Scarlet tensed, and Barbara jumped up to greet him.

"Son, I wasn't expecting you this early," Barbara said, her voice shaky. "Dinner won't be ready for a while."

Bobby's gaze raked over Scarlet then Ray, a sardonic look in his eyes. "I didn't know you'd invited *her*." He gestured toward Ray. "And you included one of my brothers. Now that's the real shocker."

Scarlet rubbed the tender spot on her thigh where he'd burned her with the cigarette. "Hello, Bobby."

Ray stood and extended his hand. "This is obviously awkward for both of us, Bobby, but I figured it's time we met."

"Yeah, about damn time." Bobby stared at Ray's proffered hand, but didn't accept the invitation to shake. "Now what is it you really want?"

Bobby strode toward the bar table by the fireplace and poured himself a drink. He didn't bother to offer Ray one, but leaned against the bar, animosity radiating from him. "You wanted to meet the illegitimate black sheep of the family?"

"I wanted to meet you, yes. I didn't know about you until Scarlet told me."

"Yeah, you can always depend on Scarlet to insert herself in the middle of family business."

His resentment rang through loud and clear, but Ray refused to indulge Bobby's self-pity. They were not going to make friends here, so he chose to be direct. "Where were you last night, Bobby?"

A muscle ticked in Bobby's jaw. "Why do you wanna know?"

"Did you go to Horseshoe Creek after you left my house, Bobby?" Scarlet asked.

Bobby tossed back his drink, but before he could speak, Barbara cleared her throat. "Bobby was with me."

Bobby jerked his head toward Barbara, then a grin curved his mouth. "That's right." He crossed the room and slung his arm around his mother's shoulders. "Mom and I had dinner and watched a movie, didn't we?"

"Yes," Barbara said with a tight smile. "I cooked Bobby's favorite chicken-fried steak."

Scarlet doubted that. Bobby had never stayed home with his mother when she lived with them. He was always out on the prowl.

Bobby rubbed his belly. "Dad always loved Mom's home cooking. She makes the best huckleberry pie in Wyoming."

Scarlet wanted to slap her brother for being so rude. He was intentionally trying to hurt Ray.

"Now, Ray," Bobby said as he took a menacing step toward Ray. "I have stuff to do. You got something you came here to say, say it."

Ray gestured toward the door. "Why don't we talk outside for a minute?"

Barbara looked panicked, so Scarlet tried to play mediator. "It's okay, Barbara. Ray just wants to discuss Joe's will."

Barbara's eyes flickered with surprise. "I see. He came here to try to buy us out of our share."

So she *had* received notification from the lawyer.

"That's not true," Ray said.

Barbara fidgeted. "Whether you and your brothers like it or not, Bobby was Joe's son," she said. "He lost out all his life. He deserves what Joe left him and you aren't going to deprive him of one damn cent."

"THAT'S NOT MY INTENTION," Ray said, although Bobby and Barbara were definitely a complication in his life.

Bobby squeezed his mother's arm. "Let me handle this, Mom."

Ray stepped outside with Bobby, braced for a

confrontation. Storm clouds rolled in, darkening the sky, matching his mood.

Any man who hit or threatened a woman was a bully and a coward. McCullen men had been taught to respect and protect women, as well as those smaller and weaker than them, especially from people like this scumbag.

He's your half brother. Joe's other son, his flesh and blood.

It didn't matter.

Or did it? Could Bobby be redeemed?

"Scarlet told me that the three of you are named in the will," Ray began.

"Mom was right. You came to pay me off so I won't show up and burst your family's happy little bubble."

Ray ground his teeth. "My family doesn't live in a bubble. We've had our share of problems, but we don't take our frustrations out on women."

Bobby's nostrils flared. "You don't know what it's like to be the kid your daddy hid."

"Is that the reason you set fire to our barns?"

Bobby's lip curled into a sneer. "I don't know what you're talking about."

"That's right. You were here last night with your mother, weren't you?"

"You're damn right. Besides," Bobby said in a sinister voice, "if I'm named in the will, why would I go making trouble before the reading?

I'm not stupid. I want to know if my father finally did right by me."

He had a point. Unless Bobby had some idea what had been left to him and he was ticked off about not getting more.

Ray squared his shoulders. "You'd better be telling the truth, because if I find out you set that fire, you're going to jail. And you'll never see a penny of that inheritance."

Bobby jerked him by the collar. "Listen to me, McCullen, your daddy screwed me over as a kid. He'd better not screw me over now that he's dead. And if you try to stop me from getting what's mine, you'll be sorry."

Ray met his gaze with a warning one, then he gripped Bobby's hand and peeled his fingers away. "Touch me again and *you'll* be sorry." He gestured toward the house where he could see Scarlet through the window. "About Scarlet—"

"My relationship with her is none of your business."

Ray gave him a menacing look. "I'm making it my business. Touch Scarlet again, and I'll kill you."

"WELL, I TAKE it that didn't go too well," Scarlet said as they drove away.

Ray clenched the steering wheel. "Bobby is a coward and a bully. If he hurts you or threatens you again, let me know."

Scarlet's heart fluttered. "Ray, you don't have to go to war for me. I can handle Bobby."

He gave her a dark look, emotions glittering in his eyes. "He may be blood related to our family, but he's not a McCullen. My daddy taught us never to hurt a woman or child."

"Joe tried to teach him that, too," Scarlet said. "And Bobby pretended like he followed the rules. Until Joe wasn't around."

"Like I said, he's a coward."

Her cell phone buzzed as he drove toward her house, and she checked the caller ID. It was a text from Hugh asking her to dinner. She'd turned him down so many times she thought he'd get the message. She quickly texted back that she was busy.

"Who is that?" Ray asked.

Scarlet shrugged. "My coworker."

"Is there a problem?"

"No."

Silence fell thick for a minute. "You know we didn't talk about old boyfriends," Ray said quietly. "Is there someone in your past who would have cut your brake lines to get back at you for some reason? Someone other than Bobby?"

Scarlet's face flushed. "There aren't any old boyfriends, Ray."

Another heartbeat of silence, and she shifted, wishing she'd worded her answer differently. She didn't want Ray to see her as a total misfit.

"Bobby hates me more than anyone. Although Lloyd Pullman has his reasons, too."

"The deputy has a BOLO out for him," Ray said. "Hopefully he'll pick him up, and if he cut those lines, he'll go to prison. Then you won't have to worry about him anymore."

No, but she'd still worry about his little girl until the child's grandparents were granted custody. Children needed parents, even if they weren't available all the time. They needed to feel loved.

Ray made a sound in his throat. "You know as much as I dislike Bobby, his argument made sense. Why would he sabotage us or the ranch before he learns what he inherited? Not only would he be hurting himself, but he's risking jail when he stands to have a piece of Horseshoe Creek."

Scarlet contemplated what he'd said. "That's true. Although sometimes when Bobby's drinking, he simply reacts instead of behaving rationally."

"I can see that," Ray agreed.

"How about other enemies Joe might have made? He was well-known in the ranching community."

"True. And Maddox just arrested a cattle-rustling ring. We're looking into some men associated with that."

They reached her house, and he turned down the drive. Her head was throbbing now, the day's events wearing on her. An image of her Wrangler diving into that brick building flashed back, and she shivered and reached for the door.

Ray caught her arm before she got out. "Are you sure you're all right?"

"Yes. I'm just tired and I have a headache."

Ray gently lifted her chin with his thumb and forced her to look into his eyes. Her heart fluttered again at the tender concern in his expression. "Call me if you need anything."

His gruff voice made tears burn her eyes. For a moment, heat flared between them, and she felt suddenly drawn to Ray. He was more like Joe than he realized. Of course, Joe had been a father figure.

Ray was no father figure; at least not to her. He was…sexy. Strong. Protective. A tough cowboy who made her think of kisses on a long hot Wyoming night. Of touches that weren't fatherly or brotherly, but titillating.

Her gaze zeroed in on his mouth, and she had the insane desire to kiss him.

He leaned forward, and she did the same, her body aching to be held, her lips craving the feel of his. His lingered near hers, his gaze darkening, as if he was torn.

His heavy sigh echoed in the air—a sigh filled with need, desire, hunger…doubt.

She should pull away. Stop this insanity before it got started.

But their lips touched, and Scarlet closed her eyes and lost herself in the moment.

HUNGER BOLTED THROUGH Ray as Scarlet's lips touched his. God help him, he couldn't resist.

He cupped her face in his hands and deepened the kiss, savoring the sweet taste of her desire. She lifted one hand to his shoulder, and he thought she was going to push him away. She *should* push him away, *dammit*.

But she stroked his arm instead as if she craved his warmth and strength, igniting his own need to protect and comfort her. She had been through hell today. She could have died in that accident.

And she was still in danger.

That realization brought reality crashing back. He had no business touching her. Kissing her. Wanting her.

His own father had considered her a daughter. Which made them what—almost half brother and half sister?

But they weren't related, and he hadn't grown up in the same house with her as an adopted sibling. She was nothing but a stranger.

Albeit a desirable, sexy one that was getting under his skin.

That realization made him pull away.

Passion lingered in Scarlet's gaze, her lips were swollen from his kiss, her face flushed with passion. He dropped his hands to his sides and balled them into fists to keep from pulling her toward him again.

He couldn't get involved with her. Maddox and Brett didn't know about Barbara, much less her or Bobby.

No telling how they would react. It would be even worse if he slept with Scarlet.

Slept with her? Yeah, that was where this was going.

He had to put a stop to it before he crossed the line.

Chapter Eleven

Scarlet's body tingled with need as Ray pulled away from her. Why had he stopped?

That kiss was…tender and erotic, and she wanted it to go on forever.

"I'm sorry, Scarlet." Self-deprecation tinged his voice. "I shouldn't have done that."

Confusion washed over Scarlet, along with the feeling that she had done something wrong. Barbara's crude accusation about cozying up with Ray to get something from him taunted her. "No, I'm sorry, Ray. I…didn't mean to come on to you."

Ray's look darkened. "You didn't. It was me. I…it's just been a tense day."

"Yes, it has been." Although kissing him had soothed her anxiety and made her body hum with a different kind of tension. One that could bring them both pleasure.

"This thing between us is just…"

"Natural," Scarlet said softly. At least it was for

her. And she was not the kind of girl who slept around. She could think of maybe one other man who'd made her feel hot from just a look.

And that had ended disastrously.

So would this if she allowed it to continue.

He removed his black Stetson and scraped his hand through his hair. "I was going to say it's complicated."

Silence stretched between them thick and unsettling. "I know. I…"

"Feel like we're almost family?" Ray asked.

Scarlet frowned. "No. You and I aren't related, Ray."

"Yeah, but my father thought of you as the daughter he never had."

Scarlet didn't know how to respond to that. "I understand that bothers you, but Joe had a big heart. The fact that Joe took me in and cared for me doesn't diminish the love he had for you and your brothers."

Ray released a weary breath. "Maybe not. But he should have had the guts to come clean before he died."

She supposed she couldn't blame him for being bitter. Joe had put them all in an uncomfortable spot. The man had a heart of gold, but dealing with confrontation was his weakness.

"You're right. I…wish Joe had told you about me and Barbara and Bobby."

Pain flashed in Ray's eyes. "So do I. I don't

know how my brothers are going to react, but I owe them the truth."

She wet her lips with her tongue, but she could still taste Ray's heady flavor. She wanted more.

Of course, Ray might have a girlfriend. He was virile, sexy, a single bachelor. For all she knew he might even be engaged or have a child somewhere.

Ray's phone buzzed and he checked the caller ID. "It's Deputy Whitefeather. I'd better answer this."

Scarlet tugged her jacket around her and lifted a hand to wave goodbye, then hurried to her front door. If she didn't let Ray go now, she might invite him inside.

With her body still aching for him, that would not be a good idea. She didn't want him to think she was trying to seduce him because she had her own agenda.

RAY WATCHED SCARLET go inside her house with mixed emotions. Hunger still heated his blood.

But he had done the right thing by calling a halt to that kiss.

"Ray," Deputy Whitefeather said. "I haven't been able to locate Pullman. He's not at his apartment or job."

"Where does he work?"

"A fertilizer plant. His boss said he's going to can him if he doesn't come in tomorrow."

Another thing the man would be ticked off

about. Abusers generally laid the blame for their faults on everyone else.

He glanced back at Scarlet's, wondering if he should stay and watch her house in case Bobby or Pullman showed up.

"I called his cell and left a message for him to check in with me. I told him if he didn't, I'd issue a warrant for his arrest."

"Did you find out anything from Scarlet's car?"

"Not yet. I dusted the brake lines and car for prints, but didn't find anything useful. Whoever cut those lines must have worn gloves."

Smug bastard probably thought he'd get away with it. But Ray would find out who'd tried to kill Scarlet.

"I met Bobby Lowman, Scarlet's adopted brother." Even though he'd only just learned about Bobby, a smidgen of guilt nagged at Ray for implicating his own half brother in a crime. "It's possible he had something to do with her crash. They've had differences over the years. And he has a rap sheet."

"I'll do a background check on him," Deputy Whitefeather offered.

Ray thanked him, but kept silent about his relationship to Bobby. Although Bobby had made a valid point about motive, Ray still wasn't ready to dismiss him as a suspect in the fire.

"Since you mentioned Arlis Bennett offered

to buy Horseshoe Creek, I thought I'd have a talk with Bennett myself."

"I'll meet you at his place," Ray said.

"I don't know if that's such a good idea, Ray."

"I don't care." Ray started the engine and headed toward the Circle T, Boyle Gates's spread. "If he wants my daddy's land and is trying to push us into selling, I have a right to confront him face-to-face."

"All right, Ray, but let me do the talking," Whitefeather said. "I don't want this to turn into something bad. Maddox wouldn't like it if I had to arrest his brother."

Ray grimaced. Except Bobby was their brother, too, and if he had sabotaged them or tried to kill Scarlet, they would arrest him anyway.

SCARLET SWALLOWED A painkiller for her headache and had just laid down hoping for a nap when her doorbell dinged. Almost asleep, she silently willed whomever it was to go away.

Although Ray might have returned…

Her heartbeat picked up at the thought. Foolish of her. She and Ray and his brothers and Bobby had a messy situation to contend with.

She traced a finger over the porcelain doll Joe had given her and grief nearly overwhelmed her. It was painful enough to lose her surrogate father. She didn't need to fall in love with his son.

Keeping her heart intact was something she

had to do in order to survive. And Scarlet was a survivor.

The doorbell dinged again, and she threw aside the blue-and-green Handmade by Willow quilt she'd bought at Vintage Treasures, and rubbed her eyes as she padded to the living room.

"Scarlet, it's me, Hugh. Let me in."

She groaned. More than anything she wanted to be alone right now, but she knew Hugh well enough to realize that if he was worried, he wouldn't leave without seeing for himself that she was all right.

They had met at the orphanage when they were kids, and he'd glued himself to her side. He was upset when she moved in with Barbara and Joe, but they'd stayed friends. Later when she went to college, she had encouraged him to get a degree and he'd surprised her by following in her footsteps.

When he'd landed the job at Social Services, they had reconnected.

But he wanted more. He'd hinted at it several times.

Unfortunately he wasn't her type.

No. Big, tough, dark-eyed, Stetson-wearing cowboys were her type. Men like Ray.

Lord help me.

"Scarlet?"

"I'm coming," she called as she unlatched the door. When she pushed it open, he stood on the other side, his reddish-brown hair in a mass of messy curls where he'd rammed his hands through it. One of his nervous habits that he hadn't been able to break.

"I'm so glad to see you," he said as he elbowed his way inside. "I've been worried sick about you."

Scarlet closed the door and followed him to her den. The room was chilly, so she lit a fire, grabbed the afghan off the sofa and wrapped it around her as she sank onto the couch. It might be rude, but she didn't intend to offer him a drink or even coffee because that would only prolong the visit.

"I told you on the phone that I was all right," Scarlet said. "Thank you for talking to the Fullers."

"No problem. It's all set with the judge for the final hearing."

Relief surged through Scarlet. "Then little Corey will finally have his family and can begin healing."

Hugh studied her, his hazel eyes more astute than she'd like at the moment. He could always tell when she was upset or worried.

"The crash wasn't accidental, was it?"

She shook her head. "No. My brake lines were cut. The deputy sheriff is investigating."

Shock widened Hugh's eyes. "It was that Lloyd Pullman, wasn't it? He's a violent man."

Scarlet shrugged, reluctant to point fingers at anyone. What if she named Pullman or Bobby and they hadn't cut her brakes? "I don't know yet, Hugh."

"Didn't Pullman threaten you when you removed his daughter from his home?"

"Yes, and he's out on bail," Scarlet said. "So be careful, Hugh. If he shows up at the office or anywhere else, do not engage with him."

"I won't, and neither should you." He studied the pictures on the mantel. When he turned to her, questions flared in his eyes. "Who was that man you were with earlier?"

Scarlet's pulse hammered. "How do you know I was with someone?"

Hugh's gaze darted sideways as if he was nervous. Another one of his tells. "He showed up at your office after the accident. And he brought you home, didn't he?"

An uneasy feeling rippled through Scarlet. "You were watching?"

"No. I mean I drove over and happened to see you get out of the car."

Had Hugh seen her kiss Ray? She wrapped the afghan tighter around her. She didn't know how to begin to explain her relationship with Ray. Especially since that kiss. "That was Ray McCullen, Joe McCullen's youngest son."

His brows climbed his forehead. "I wasn't aware you knew the brothers."

"I don't. Not really." Although she had kissed Ray and wanted to kiss him again. But his brothers would probably hate her when they discovered who she was. And there might be a court battle...

"But I had to meet them because of Joe's will."

"He included you?"

"Yes. And Bobby."

Hugh grunted. "Let me guess. The McCullens didn't know about you or Bobby and they aren't too happy about his will."

Scarlet couldn't deny the obvious. "No, they didn't know about us. Ray does now, though."

"Do you think he'd hurt you?"

Scarlet bit back a laugh. Ray McCullen might be dangerous to her heart, but he was like Joe through and through. The one thing she was sure of was that he respected women.

Still, he and his brothers might try to exclude her from Joe's inheritance.

"No, Hugh, Ray won't hurt me. I think it was probably Pullman or Bobby who cut the brake lines. But I'm fine now, and the deputy is investigating." She stood. "I have a headache and would like to rest."

Hugh touched her shoulder. "Let me stay, Scarlet. I can watch out, make sure no one bothers you."

She couldn't sleep with Hugh in her house. He was making her more and more uncomfortable. "Thank you. I appreciate the offer. But the most important thing you can do to help me is to man the office and make sure things are running smoothly there. I don't want anything to ruin Corey's placement."

"Of course I'll do that. But..."

The concern in his eyes hadn't faltered. "But what? Is there something you're not telling me?"

He shifted and jammed his hands in his pockets with a sigh. "I'm sorry, Scarlet. I wanted to take care of this for you, but I decided you ought to see it."

Scarlet's shoulders knotted with tension. "See what?"

Hugh pulled an envelope from his jacket and handed it to her. Scarlet noted her name on the outside spelled with letters cut from a magazine.

"You opened it?"

"It wasn't sealed, and when I saw those cutout letters, I got worried. So I looked inside. It's not pretty, Scarlet. It's downright scary."

Scarlet took a deep breath and opened the envelope, then gasped. There was a picture of her taken from a distance as she exited her office.

Then another photo—except in this one her face had been crossed out with a black marker and the edges had been seared.

Chapter Twelve

Ray studied Arlis Bennett as he and Deputy Whitefeather seated themselves in the man's office. Bennett was Boyle Gates's cousin and seemed to have moved right into the Circle T, apparently hoping to keep Gates's operation running smoothly in his absence.

"You come to check up on me?" Bennett asked the deputy.

Ray scanned the room, noting the dark furnishings, photographs of Gates holding an award he'd won for his beef, then the ashtray on Bennett's desk. Was he a smoker?

"I thought we should talk." Deputy Whitefeather maintained a neutral expression, which Ray was beginning to realize was normal for the Native American. His wide jaw and high cheekbones framed dark, intense eyes that seemed to view everyone in the world with suspicion.

Bennett steepled his big beefy hands on top of the massive desk. "Do I need my lawyer?"

"I don't know, do you?" Deputy Whitefeather asked.

Ray liked the way the deputy operated. He was so still and calm that it was unnerving.

Bennett shifted. "No. My cousin asked me to move in and take care of things while he's away."

"You mean while he's incarcerated," the deputy pointed out.

Bennett's jaw twitched. "Yes. But if you've looked into my background, and I'm sure you have, you know I'm clean."

"Boyle appeared to be clean, too," Ray pointed out, "but he took advantage of his ranch hands, my father and other ranchers in the area."

Bennett's ruddy face formed a scowl. "As I said, I'm here to clean up the business. You decide to take me up on my offer?"

Ray squared his shoulders. "No, my brothers and I aren't interested in selling any part of Horseshoe Creek. That land stands for family." He'd fight for the McCullen legacy if he had to.

Bennett drummed his fingers on the desk. "Let me know if you change your mind."

"We won't," Ray said firmly. "Although I believe someone might be trying to sabotage our plans to expand."

Bennett's bushy eyebrows drew together. "What are you talking about?"

"Someone set fire to the new barns we were building," Ray said.

Bennett made a low sound in his throat. "*Good God*, you think I'm responsible?"

Ray met the man's stare head-on. "I don't know. Are you?"

Bennett stood, jowls shaking as he clenched his jaw. "That's ridiculous. Just because my cousin crossed you, you have no right to accuse me of arson. Besides," he said, his voice rising with irritation, "maybe you set the fire so you could frame me and destroy the Circle T. If you run us out of business, Horseshoe Creek will prosper even more."

Ray shot up, furious. "That is ridiculous."

The deputy laid a hand on Ray's shoulder to keep him from attacking the man. "Bennett, where were you last night?"

Bennett glared at both of them, then flattened his palms on the desk and leaned forward, cheeks bulging. "I had dinner at the Cattleman's Club. You can ask the other twenty-five people there."

Ray gritted his teeth. He was making an enemy of Bennett, and for business's sake that wasn't a good idea. But he had to know the truth.

"You could have hired someone to set the fire," Ray said.

Bennett cursed and swung a thumb toward the door. "I'm through with your accusations and insults. Get out, McCullen."

"I would like to speak to your hands," Deputy Whitefeather said.

Bennett went very still, his calm demeanor returning, although his voice held barely controlled rage. "Then get a damn warrant."

"I don't need a warrant to have a conversation with them," Deputy Whitefeather said in a tone that brooked no argument.

A vein throbbed in Bennett's forehead. "Then I'll call my attorney."

Whitefeather shrugged. "Fine, if you have something to hide, go ahead."

Bennett picked up the phone on his desk. "I don't have anything to hide, but I don't intend to be railroaded for something I didn't do or let you ruin my reputation." He glared at McCullen. "You're going to regret this, McCullen."

"That sounds like a threat," Ray said.

"Take it however you want to take it. But when the other ranchers around here find out you're pointing fingers at the locals, no one is going to be your friend."

Ray understood the threat now. Bennett would blackball the McCullens in the ranching community, and that wouldn't be good.

Two could play that game. "You think they trust you after what your cousin did?" Ray asked.

Bennett's face heated. He knew Ray was right. But had he or one of his people set that fire?

"Print me a list of your employees and call them

together," Deputy Whitefeather said. "If you have nothing to hide, I'll be out of your hair in an hour or two."

Bennett muttered another curse, called his foreman, clicked a few keys and hit Print, then handed the deputy a list.

"I'm going with you to talk to my men," Bennett said.

Whitefeather stood. "Then let's get to it."

Ray wanted to accompany them, but his phone was buzzing. Brett. He snatched it up. "Yeah?"

"Gus Garcia wants to meet with us. He might have a lead on the arsonist."

SCARLET STARED AT the picture, fear mingling with shock. She flipped the envelope over and searched for an address or postal address. Except for her name, though, the envelope was blank.

"Where did you get this?" she asked Hugh.

"It was on the floor when I returned from lunch today. Someone slipped it under the door."

"Did you see anyone hanging around the office who could have left it?"

Hugh jammed his hands in his pockets. "No. The Fullers were the only ones who stopped by today."

"How about a strange car? Maybe in the parking lot or down the street."

"I didn't see anything," Hugh said, his voice slightly defensive. "If I had, I'd tell you, Scarlet."

"I know you would, Hugh. I'm just trying to figure out who left this. It might be the same person who cut my brake lines."

"Are you going to give it to the sheriff?"

Scarlet laid the envelope on the table by the sofa. "He's out of town, but I'll show it to Deputy Whitefeather. Maybe he can lift some prints from the envelope or picture."

Although she doubted he left prints. Whoever had sent this was clever and had probably worn gloves.

Hugh reached for her hand and pulled it into his. "I know this is scary, Scarlet. I'll be happy to stay here with you. You shouldn't be alone tonight."

Uncomfortable with the possessive look in his eyes, Scarlet squeezed his hand, then pulled away. "Thank you, Hugh, but I'm exhausted and really want to rest."

He gestured toward the sofa. "I'll stay out here."

"Hugh," Scarlet said, her voice firm as she led him to the door. "It's been a really difficult day, and I need to be alone. I'll see you at the office tomorrow."

He stood in the doorway for a few more seconds, lingering, obviously hoping she'd change her mind, but the longer he stalled, the more irritated she became.

"There is something you can do for me," she

said, anxious to smooth over the tension. "Please open up the office in the morning. I'll be in after I drop this envelope at the sheriff's office."

He finally agreed and left. Scarlet locked the door, then watched him drive away, but just as she was about to head back to bed, lights flickered along the street.

She couldn't make out the type of car, but it slowed as it passed her yard, and suddenly the window slid down, giving her a view of the man's face.

Pullman.

"WHAT DO YOU think about Bennett?" Ray asked as Deputy Whitefeather walked him to his vehicle.

"I don't like him, but we need proof that he's done something illegal," Whitefeather said. "He could easily have paid someone to set the fire. I'll look into his financials."

"Does he have a record?"

"Nothing that I've found. But I'll keep digging." He gestured toward the man who was standing on his front porch watching them. "He's definitely suspicious, though."

"Let me know what happens with his hands. Brett called. I'm meeting him to talk to one of our men who might have information about the fire."

They shook hands and agreed to stay in touch. Ray jumped in his Range Rover and drove back toward Horseshoe Creek. The dark clouds thickened, casting a grayness to the land as night set in.

He wondered what Scarlet was doing, if she was resting. If she was safe.

Dammit, he shouldn't care so much.

He veered down the drive to the ranch, scanning the pastures and stables in search of trouble. The memory of those flames shooting in the sky haunted him.

The scent of smoke still lingered in the air as he drove past the burn site. Crime scene tape roped off the area, a reminder of the violence against them. Brett had moved the animals to another stable nearer to the main house.

They couldn't chance one of their horses being injured or...worse.

Sweat broke out on his brow at the very thought. Cruelty to animals ranked almost as high as cruelty to women and kids.

Brett had suggested they meet at Brett's cabin to keep other hands from suspecting that Garcia might be ratting one of them out.

Brett's wife, Willow, was outside playing horseshoes with Sam, the son she and Brett had had together. She looked up and waved, and he got out of his SUV, strode over and ruffled Sam's hair.

"Looks like your daddy's teaching you to be a pro," he said.

Sam grinned and tossed the horseshoe. "He gave me a riding lesson this morning."

"You'll be in the rodeo before you know it."

Willow shook her finger at him. "Don't start that, Ray."

He chuckled, enjoying the light moment, and glad Brett had finally come home.

Maybe it was time he returned for good, too.

He froze, wondering where that thought had come from. He was a rambling man. His detective work took him wherever the case led.

No ties. No one to question him.

Or to love him.

Although love had never been high on his priority list.

Brett appeared on the porch and waved him in. "See you in a bit, Sam. Keep practicing and we'll have a McCullen tournament."

Sam high-fived him, then Ray climbed the porch. Garcia was already inside with a cup of coffee when Ray entered.

"You remember Ray, Gus?"

"Yes, sir." Gus stood, wiped his hands on his jeans and shook Ray's hand. Brett had told him about Gates setting Garcia up for cattle rustling, and that the leader of the gang had threatened to hurt Garcia's family if he ratted out the real rustlers. Thankfully, Brett had convinced Garcia to talk and he'd given Garcia's family protection.

Once the arrests were made, Maddox had offered Gus a job on the ranch.

"You have information about the fire?" Brett said.

Gus rubbed his jaw with work-roughened hands. "I don't like to speak bad about the men. Most of them work hard and are like me, they need the jobs."

"I understand that you've had it tough, Gus," Ray said. "And trust me, no one will know that you talked to us. But our horses could have been killed in that fire."

"*Sí*, I understand." Gus spread his hands on the table and looked down at them. "I'm sorry, but I don't know who set the fire."

"Then why did you want to see us?" Ray asked.

"There is someone who has a grudge against your family."

Brett patted his back. "Who are you talking about?"

Gus sipped his coffee as they seated themselves around the table. Ray tapped his foot on the floor as they waited on Gus to talk.

He drummed his fingers on his leg. "One of the new hands, Marvin Hardwick, he used to work for Boyle Gates."

Ray and Brett straightened. "Hardwick, he's one of the guys I pointed out to you when we met at the dining hall, isn't he, Brett? He was smoking outside."

"Yeah, the other guy was Stan Romley. I looked at their employment files but they seemed clean."

Of course they could have faked information, Ray thought.

"You're sure Hardwick worked with Gates?" Brett asked.

"Yes, sir." Gus lifted his head, the mole at the corner of his mouth twitching as his lips thinned. "He worked for Gates when they framed me for the cattle rustling."

"Did he help set you up?" Brett asked.

Gus shrugged. "I don't know, and it don't matter now. But I heard him talking about those barns. He said he rode out there to check on the progress."

The chair legs rattled as Brett pushed back from the table. "I'm going to get him and make him talk."

Ray's phone buzzed. He checked the number. Scarlet.

He started to ignore it. He and Brett had work to do here. They finally had a lead. Although someone had tried to kill Scarlet earlier, so he couldn't ignore the call.

He excused himself and punched Connect. "Scarlet, I—"

"Ray, it's that man Pullman. He's outside my house."

Ray's heart stuttered with panic. "Keep the doors locked. I'll be right there."

Chapter Thirteen

Rain began to splatter the windshield, and the wind picked up, shaking the trees with its force as Ray drove toward Scarlet's. Another car zoomed up on his tail, and Ray cursed as the headlights blinded him.

He tapped his brakes to signal to the driver to get off his tail, but the car sped up instead. Clenching the steering wheel in a white-knuckled grip, Ray pressed the accelerator, maneuvering the Range Rover around a curve.

The car accelerated as well, riding him so close that Ray thought he was going to ram into him. Furious, he spotted a dirt road to the side and steered his vehicle onto it, his tires churning over gravel and rock as he tried to slow.

But he hit a slick patch and skidded, a boulder coming toward him. Determined not to collide with it, he swung the steering wheel to the right and barely missed it, then skidded another few feet until he lurched to a stop only inches away from a thicket of trees.

Breathing hard, he checked his rearview mirror, searching for the car, then cursed again when he spotted it barreling toward him.

Ray's instincts surged to life. He needed his gun.

He reached for the dash to unlock it, but suddenly the car slammed into his rear, jarring him. Cursing again, he scrambled to reach the gun, but before he could unlock the dash, a hulking man yanked open his door and jerked him from the SUV. Ray raised his fist to punch the man and tried to get a look at his face, but it was so damn dark and rainy all he could see was a shadow.

The man dodged the blow, then shoved Ray to the ground on his knees. He heaved a breath, spun around and rammed the man in the belly with his head, hoping to knock him backward. This SOB wasn't going to get the best of him.

Ray knew how to fight.

But just as he tackled him, something slammed into his lower back. Metal. A tire iron?

Pain screamed through his kidneys, and he dug his hands into the muddy ground to steady himself. Before he could recover, another blow came, this one higher. The blow knocked the wind from his lungs and sent him sprawling on the ground.

He spit out dirt and mud, swaying as he pushed

himself up to fight. He grabbed the man's ankle, hoping to slam his fists into his knee and bring him down, but another blow from the tire iron to his kidneys sent him writhing in pain again.

Taking advantage of the moment, the bastard kicked the hell out of him. His boots pounded into Ray's back, then his knees. Ray struggled to breathe through the pain and get up, but the man had the strength of three men and knew where to hit.

Ray rolled to the side to dodge another blow, but the tire iron connected with the side of his head. Shock from the blow disoriented him.

He inhaled and grabbed at the man's legs to pull him down, but the tire iron caught him on the side of the head again and Ray collapsed.

He fought to stay conscious but he lost the battle, and the damn world went black.

SCARLET WATCHED THROUGH the window as Pullman slowed his truck and parked on the street. He had chosen a strategic spot giving him a view of her house.

Was he going to break in, or did he just want to frighten her?

Rain drizzled down, and he rolled the window up slightly, leaving it open just enough so she could see his menacing face in the shadows of the streetlight.

The tip of his cigarette glowed bright orange in the dark, smoke curling out the window and disappearing into the fog.

She inhaled sharply, determined not to succumb to panic. Ray was on his way. She was safe in the house.

Still…she rushed to her nightstand and retrieved her gun, then returned to the window.

In spite of her resolve to be strong, fear nearly choked her. He was gone. Not inside the truck.

Was he going to break into the house?

Heart pounding, she pushed back the curtain and scanned the street. He wasn't in front of the truck. Or at the rear.

She searched around the car, then her yard, but she didn't spot him anywhere. Sweating now, she inched to the door and peeked through the peephole.

Nothing.

A noise echoed from the back, and she startled, tightening her fingers around the gun handle. Forcing herself to be very still so she could hear, she listened for sounds of an intruder. The rain was coming down steadily now, the wind rattling the house.

Suddenly something banged the window in the back. A tree limb? Or was it Pullman?

A bead of perspiration trickled down the back of her neck as she inched through the living room and peered into the hallway leading to the laundry room and back door.

The wind whistled through the eaves of the house. Then another noise. Someone jiggling the door knob?

Terrified and praying Ray showed up soon, she gripped the gun at the ready. If Pullman tried to hurt her, she would shoot him.

A thumping started at the back door, and she held the gun in front of her, aiming it at eye level. If he was inside, she wanted him to realize she was armed.

Glass shattered, and her panic mushroomed.

"I have a gun," she called out. "And I'm not afraid to use it."

Suddenly the lights flickered off, pitching her into the dark. The scent of her own fear pervaded the air, and she fought a scream as a noise erupted behind her.

Back in the living room? How...

She couldn't wait on Ray. She snatched her phone from her pocket to call 911. A knock at the front door made her jump again.

It was loud, pounding.

Her hand trembled as she inched back to the front room. The knock sounded again, louder this time.

Then she looked through the peephole and Pullman was standing on the porch, his beady eyes glaring at her through the tiny hole.

RAY SLOWLY ROUSED back to consciousness. His back throbbed and his eyes were blurry, but he blinked, the world finally sliding into focus.

Damn. Some bastard had not only run him off the road, but he'd gotten the best of him and beaten him to a pulp.

That rarely happened.

He wouldn't get away with it.

He wiped blood from his right eye that was already swollen half-shut and peered around his surroundings to make sure his attacker was gone. His Range Rover was still sitting there, but the sedan was gone.

Relieved, he pushed himself up from the dirt, wincing as pain knifed through his lower back. Hell, he'd probably be sore for days.

Mentally retracing the past hour as he stumbled back to his vehicle, he scrambled to recall details of the man's face. But it had been dark and that first blow to his kidneys had sent his world into a blur. He thought the car was black, but it could have been dark green. He hadn't seen the license plate.

Hand shaking, he wrenched the car door open and fell into the driver's side. He fumbled for the keys, then realized they weren't in the ignition and spit out an obscenity. Had his attacker taken them so he couldn't follow?

More blood trickled down the side of his face and he swiped at it with the back of his hand, then searched the seat and floor, but the keys weren't there.

Frustration screamed through him, and he turned to scan the dirt by the car. It was so dark the ground and grass blended together, so he grabbed the flashlight he kept in the backseat and used it to light a path.

Pain throbbed through his body as he searched the bushes and trees. But either the man had taken the keys with him or thrown them into the woods.

It would take all night to find them.

Time he didn't have. Scarlet had called because Pullman was outside her house. She sounded terrified. He'd been on his way to her.

He bellowed in anger. He didn't have time to search the damn woods. He needed to get to Scarlet.

He hurriedly limped back to his SUV. Seconds later, he hot-wired the vehicle, then sped onto the road, slinging gravel in his haste to turn onto the highway.

He quickly glanced left and right, looking for that car again, but the road seemed deserted. Scarlet's terrified voice echoed in his ears, and he punched the accelerator.

If Pullman had hurt her, he'd never forgive himself.

Lights nearly blinded him as a car raced toward him. He tensed, bracing himself in case his attacker had returned, but the car flew past and disappeared the other direction.

Ray reached inside his pocket and grabbed a handkerchief, then wiped at the blood on his face as he maneuvered the curves and turns until he reached Scarlet's neighborhood.

The houses were spread apart, a few lights glowing from inside, cars parked in the driveways. He spotted a pickup parked in front of Scarlet's, and slowed before he reached it, scouting out her yard in search of the man.

Not wanting to alert Pullman of his arrival, he parked two houses away. Unsure if the man was armed, he jimmied open the locked dash and grabbed his weapon. Gripping his gun, he opened his door and slid from the seat, scanning Scarlet's front yard, then the side of the house for Pullman. Woods backed up to her property, which made it a great place to hide.

Anxiety knotted his shoulders as he inched behind some bushes and crept toward Scarlet's. He spotted a shadow to the side of the house and paused, studying the movement. It went from the side to the back, then disappeared.

Gritting his teeth, he crept closer, then inched his way into Scarlet's yard, staying close to the house and bushes so Pullman wouldn't see him coming. By the time he reached the corner, Pullman had disappeared, though.

He circled the back, searching the shadows and

trees, but didn't see the man anywhere. Dammit, was he hiding back there?

He walked to the opposite side of the house, but didn't spot him, then eased his way to the front again.

Pullman stood on the front porch knocking.

What was the bastard doing? Then the truth hit him—he'd been toying with Scarlet. The sick creep wanted to terrorize her.

Keeping his gun at the ready, he inched up the front to the porch. The stairs creaked as he climbed them, and Pullman swung around.

He slowly raised his hands. "Hold on, man. Don't shoot."

Ray kept his weapon trained on the man. "You found out she survived the car crash and came here to finish her off, didn't you, you bastard?"

Pullman actually looked surprised. "What are you talking about? I came here to apologize."

"That's a lie and we both know it. You tried to kill her."

"If I'd tried to kill her, she'd be dead," Pullman said through gritted teeth.

Ray didn't know whether to believe him or not. "I think you did. And now you're trying to intimidate her."

"She took my daughter from me." Pullman's lips curved into a sneer. "I'll do whatever I have to in order to get her back."

Ray removed his phone from his pocket to call

the deputy. "Then go through the courts. And if I find evidence to prove you cut her brake lines you're going to jail for attempted murder." Ray snagged the man by the shirt. "I can have the deputy pick you up or you can get off her property now."

"Who the hell are you to tell me what to do?" Pullman snarled.

Ray gave him a lethal stare. "Someone you don't want to mess with. Now, Miss Lovett is filing a restraining order against you. If you bother her again, I'll give you a taste of your own medicine, then lock you up. And trust me, then you will never see your child again."

SCARLET HEARD VOICES echoing outside the door and looked through the peephole again. For the past half hour, Pullman had tormented her by circling her house, knocking on the windows and then running to the next one.

He wanted her to know that he could get to her.

He already was, just with his mind games.

Her breath gushed out in relief as Ray escorted the big man to his truck. Pullman slid in the seat, then gave her a sinister leer. In spite of what Ray had said, he wasn't finished with her.

Ray shoved the door shut, then Pullman took off, tires squealing as he screeched away. Scarlet hated that she was shaking and that he'd gotten to her.

But he had.

Ray strode back to the porch, his face illuminated by the streetlight. *Dear God*. His eye was bruised and swollen, his cheek purple and blood had dried on his forehead and below his eye.

She swung the door open, her heart racing. "Ray, my God, what happened to you?"

"I had an accident." He must have seen the fear in her eyes because he pulled her into his arms. She collapsed against him, so grateful to see him that she could barely breathe.

"He didn't hurt you, did he?"

"No, come on in." Forgetting her fear over Pullman, she led him through the door and ushered him to the kitchen where she could examine his injuries. He was limping slightly and winced when he sat down. She wet a washcloth in the sink, brought it to him and tilted his chin up so she could clean his wounds.

"That looks like it hurts." She gently dotted away the blood with the wet cloth. "You need a doctor, Ray. Where else are you hurt?"

He caught her hand in his and stilled her movements. "I'm just banged up, don't worry about me."

"But you're all bloody and you have a black eye." She narrowed her eyes remembering her own accident. "Tell me what happened. Did someone cut your brake lines, too?"

He shook his head, then allowed her to continue

cleaning his forehead and eye. "Some man tried to run me off the road. I veered onto a side road and managed to stop, but he followed me and beat the hell out of me." Self-derision laced his voice. "I can't believe he got the better of me."

Scarlet gently stroked his hair from his forehead. It was sweaty and sticky with blood. But at least the cut above his eye wasn't too deep.

Still, she didn't know who was shaking more, her or him. "I don't think you'll need stitches. Show me where else you're hurt."

Ray shook his head. "I told you I'm fine. I'm just sorry I was late getting here. Did Pullman try to break in?"

A shudder coursed up Scarlet's spine as she remembered his taunting. "Not exactly."

Ray took her hands in his, the worry in his eyes touching a tender chord inside her.

"What does that mean?"

Scarlet sighed and averted her eyes. More than anything she wanted Ray to wrap his arms around her again. To hold her.

Kiss her.

Stay with her tonight and keep her safe.

"Scarlet?"

"He just taunted me, Ray. He ran from window to window, banging and making noises, tapping at the windows, acting like he was going to come in."

"Sick bastard," Ray muttered. "He claims he didn't cut your brake lines, but we'll find a way to nail him. And you're going to take out a restraining order against him."

Scarlet nodded. "What about you? Did you recognize the man who attacked you?"

Ray shook his head. "No. But I'll file a police report."

Scarlet's gaze met his, the tension between them thick with worry and fear and...something else. A sexual tension she hadn't felt in a very long time.

She needed to step away. Remember all the reasons she shouldn't get involved with Ray. His brothers didn't even know about her. They had his father's will to work out.

"You should have called the deputy," Scarlet whispered.

Ray's breathing grew heavy, his gaze steeped in desire. Then he reached up and tucked a strand of hair behind her ear.

"I was too worried about you. Too afraid Pullman had broken in."

His voice triggered a warm tingling to start deep in her womb. She wet her suddenly dry lips, aching to touch him more intimately.

Ray murmured a sound of need. "Dammit, Scarlet, what are we doing here?"

"I don't know," she whispered. But she was helpless to stop the ache in her body and in her heart.

Ray must have sensed her need because he

traced a finger over her lips with one finger, then drew her to him and closed his mouth over hers.

RAY'S BODY HEATED with need as Scarlet parted her lips for him. Images of his crash, of her accident, of that maniac Pullman getting to her flashed in his head, and he deepened the kiss, desperate to feel her against him.

He needed to know she was safe.

Her lips felt soft, tender. Her body quivered against his. He stroked her back and plunged his tongue into her mouth. She sighed into him, a breathy sound filled with desire, and he lifted her hair from her neck, then trailed kisses along the smooth column of her throat.

She tilted her head back, and he tasted the sweetness of her skin, making him want more. She tossed his Stetson to the sofa, then dug her hands into his hair, and he groaned, then they walked backward to her bedroom.

Raw need consumed him, and he pressed her against the wall, then eased open the top buttons of her blouse, dropping kisses along the sensitive skin of her throat as he pushed the fabric aside. She rubbed his calf with her foot, moving her body against his in invitation.

His sex thickened, hardening at the contact, and he made quick work of the rest of the buttons, exposing a dark blue lacy bra that barely covered her breasts.

He sucked in a breath. His body ached for her like he hadn't ached for anyone in a long time.

Bruises marred her torso, from the air bag, he assumed. But a couple of other scars caught his eye. Two small round ones that looked like cigarette burns. Then a crisscross one that had probably been made by a knife.

She must have realized he was looking at them, because she covered herself with her hands. "Ray?"

"Shh, it's okay. How did you get them?"

She tried to pull away, but he pressed his body into hers. "Tell me. Was it a foster parent? Bobby?"

"Both," she said in a pained whisper.

Dammit to hell. Pure rage engulfed him, but he held himself in check. Scarlet had obviously seen her share of angry men who took their anger out on women.

He would not be one of them.

Instead, his gaze met hers, and he tried to tell her with his eyes that she could trust him. She must have read the silent promise because she lifted her head and kissed him again, this time her kiss filled with a greedy kind of hunger that invited him to love her.

He wanted her. The sex would be epic.

But if he made love to her, would he be able to walk away from her later?

Chapter Fourteen

Fueled by passion, Ray kissed her deeply, then trailed his tongue down her breasts to those scars and gently kissed each one of them. Scarlet moaned and tunneled her fingers in his hair again, as he stroked her nipples through the thin lacy barrier.

She whispered his name, and he quickly unfastened her bra, his breathing husky at the sight of her breasts spilling into his hands. Her skin was soft, her breasts full and round, her nipples perfect rosebuds.

They stiffened at his touch, making his mouth water, and he lowered his head and drew one turgid pebble into his mouth. Scarlet whispered his name on a moan, letting him know she liked it, and he suckled her until her body quivered.

She reached for the buttons on his shirt and unfastened them, then slid her hands inside, raking her nails over his chest. He inhaled at her touch, his body humming to life with erotic sensations.

Then her finger slid over his bruised ribs and he winced.

"I'm sorry, Ray."

"You can make it better," he said in a gruff voice.

His shirt fell to the floor and he walked her backward to the bed, but as they started to lie down, she shifted to move something.

A doll.

Ray froze, his heart thumping. That doll...the blond hair, big baby blue eyes...

For a moment, he felt as if he'd been sucker punched. "Where did you get that doll?"

Scarlet's eyes were glazed with passion, but his question dampened the mood. "Your father gave it to me."

Ray had no idea why that bothered him, but it did. "My mother collected those dolls," he said with a pang to his chest.

"I know," Scarlet said softly. "Joe told me about her, that she loved the dolls. That's the reason he wanted me to have one."

An image of his mother with those dolls haunted him. For some reason, it seemed wrong that his father would give away one of the few things they had left of hers. Not that he wanted the dolls, but...they had been special.

It felt like another betrayal, just as he'd felt

betrayed when he'd seen his father with Barbara as a child.

Scarlet gently touched his arm. "Ray?"

He flinched slightly. Then his phone buzzed, and he yanked it from his pocket and checked the caller ID. Brett.

Damn.

Scarlet was half naked. His body shouted for him to take her to bed and finish what they'd started.

But that doll and his brother's call reminded him what was at stake. He'd felt betrayed by his father—how would his brothers feel if they discovered they had another brother, and that he had slept with the girl Joe had considered his daughter?

The girl he'd kept secret. The one who was going to inherit part of their family legacy.

"I…" Ray grabbed his shirt and backed away. He hated himself for leaving Scarlet when she looked so beautiful. And so damn vulnerable.

His phone buzzed again, and he gestured toward it as he inched to the doorway. "I'm sorry, Scarlet. I have to take this."

She looked hurt, but she reached for her robe on the side chair. Ray left the room, feeling like a bastard.

SCARLET YANKED ON her robe and belted it, a flush creeping up her neck. She felt naked and lonely and…hurt.

What had she done wrong? Ray hadn't seemed repulsed by her scars. But the sight of that doll triggered a different reaction.

She closed her eyes, battling tears. She refused to cry over his rejection. But how dare he get her all heated up and needy, then leave her wanting more.

She tiptoed to the doorway and saw him pacing by the fireplace, his phone pressed to his ear. Maybe the phone call had been really important.

God knows they'd both almost been killed today. And the danger wasn't over. Someone was sabotaging the ranch, and Pullman wanted revenge against her.

All the more reason she needed Ray.

Needed him? The thought sent fear streaking through her. She had never needed a man before. And she couldn't allow herself to need Ray.

But this was a different kind of feeling, she silently reminded herself. She craved comfort, a pair of strong arms to lean on, a night of lovemaking to relieve the sexual tension brewing between them. Being with Ray would have reminded her they were both still alive.

Except...for that doll... The truth dawned, making her chest squeeze. It reminded him of the mother he'd lost as a child, and the fact that his father had betrayed her with Barbara.

That Joe had a second family. One who stood

to throw a monkey wrench into their family business by taking part of it.

She wasn't part of the family.

That was the reason he didn't want her to have the doll. She was not a McCullen and no matter how much Joe loved her, she never would be.

A desolate feeling overcame her.

If Ray didn't want her to have that doll, he certainly wouldn't want her to have a piece of his father's ranch.

"WHAT HAPPENED TO YOU, Ray? You ran off like something was wrong."

Ray chewed the inside of his cheek. He hated lying to his brothers and had to tell them about Bobby and Scarlet soon.

But not tonight.

"I'm sorry. I had some business to attend to, then a man came out of nowhere, ran me off the road and attacked me."

"What?" Brett's voice rose an octave. "Are you all right?"

"Yeah, just bruised." His ego had taken a beating, too.

"Do you know who it was?"

"No, a big guy, two hundred pounds, scruffy. But it was dark and he came at me so fast that I didn't get a good look at his face."

"You talk to Deputy Whitefeather about it?"

"Not yet. But I will." Scarlet had to talk to him about getting that restraining order, too.

"Why did you call, Brett?"

A heartbeat of silence passed, and Ray regretted his defensive tone. They were brothers. Brett didn't have to have a reason.

"I found Hardwick, but I haven't talked to him yet. I'm outside The Silver Bullet where I spotted his truck. I thought we might confront him together."

Ray glanced at the bedroom. In light of the night's events, he hated to leave Scarlet alone. What if Pullman returned?

Yet…if he stayed he'd be tempted to go back inside, apologize for being a jerk and ask her to give him another chance to love her.

He'd call the deputy to come over. Whitefeather could get the restraining order underway.

"I'll meet you at the bar in ten minutes."

Brett agreed, and Ray fought guilt over keeping silent about Scarlet. But he would tell Brett soon. He'd have to.

Tucking his shirt back in his jeans, he fastened his belt, retrieved his gun and Stetson and went to the bedroom and knocked. Regret needled him as Scarlet opened the door.

Pain glinted in her eyes, but she quickly lifted her head and masked it.

"That was my brother. We may have a lead on

the arsonist. I'm going to meet Brett to question the man."

"Fine."

Her curt tone told him all he needed to know. She was ticked off.

"I'll call Deputy Whitefeather and tell him about the attack on me, and about Pullman. I'll ask him to come by and get the ball rolling on the restraining order."

She gave a quick nod. "Thanks, Ray."

He hesitated, tempted to pull her against him again and assure her everything was all right. But he couldn't promise that it would be, not until he talked to his brothers.

And not until he found out the truth about the fire at the ranch.

"Scarlet, I—"

"Just go, Ray," Scarlet said. "You were right to put a halt to things."

Her look dared him to argue. He couldn't. He agreed with her.

But that didn't mean he liked it. Hell, he still wanted her with a vengeance.

SCARLET PROMISED RAY she'd keep the doors locked until the deputy arrived.

But she was seething inside. She might understand Ray's hesitation over sleeping with her. And she should be grateful he'd left. But her body still tingled with need.

She wasn't the kind of girl who slept around. In fact, she'd actually climbed into bed with only two men in her life. Well, not men. Boys.

Once at seventeen when she'd first entered college, and she was young and foolish and thought she was in love. But she was inexperienced and happily-ever-after to her meant exclusivity and marriage. To him it had meant sex with no hassles.

The second time, she was twenty-one and had dated a prosecutor, but he'd decided to join a law firm that focused on defending hardened criminals. He'd wanted the money—and she hadn't been able to stomach the people he represented. Not after the violence and abuse she'd seen in her own life and through her work.

She made a cup of tea to settle her nerves, then heard the rumble of an engine and hurried to the window to make sure Pullman hadn't returned.

The deputy's car rolled to a stop and turned in the drive. Relieved, she set her tea on the coffee table, then unlocked the door.

Deputy Whitefeather looked solemn as he strode up the steps. "Miss Lovett, Ray McCullen called and said you had trouble."

"Yes." She gestured for him to come in. "I need a restraining order against Lloyd Pullman."

"Tell me what happened."

She offered him some coffee, but he declined. So she led him to the den, explained the circumstances with Pullman's daughter and described the way the man had tormented her earlier.

The twisted man didn't realize that by threatening her he'd hurt his chances of regaining his child.

RAY SPOTTED BRETT'S truck when he pulled into the packed parking lot of The Silver Bullet.

Brett met him in the parking lot as he climbed from his SUV.

His brother caught his arm and frowned. "Hell, man, you *did* take a beating."

Ray had forgotten about his black eye and the bruises. "Don't remind me." He should have been faster to his gun.

"You been inside?" Ray asked.

Brett shook his head. "Figured I might need backup."

Ray nodded, and they walked into the bar together. Cigarette smoke clogged the air, and the room smelled of beer and whiskey. Country music was piped through the speakers, some sad song about a man losing a woman, which made him think of Scarlet.

Except Scarlet was not his woman and never would be.

Laughter and conversation echoed from the bar and a dart game was underway in the back corner. Two biker-looking dudes occupied the pool table.

Ray swept his gaze through the crowded room,

and Brett nudged his elbow, then gestured toward a young man in his twenties with a goatee, cowboy hat and boots. The watch on his left arm looked expensive, and so did the signet ring he wore on his right hand.

Cowboys didn't usually make that kind of money. Maybe he'd earned his by working for the enemy.

Brett started toward the bar and Ray followed. He strode to the opposite side of the man while Brett moved in on the other. The man had just tossed back a shot and ordered another.

Brett indicated that he and Ray wanted a shot, and the bartender set three on the bar.

Hardwick went to pick up his glass, and Brett laid a hand on his shoulder. "We need to talk, man."

Ray set a hand on the other. "Yeah, Hardwick."

Panic flashed in Hardwick's eyes, the kind born of guilt. He slid off the barstool and sprinted through the crowd, pushing people in his haste to escape.

"Dammit," Brett muttered.

Ray cursed, too, then took off running.

Chapter Fifteen

"I can't believe he's running!" Brett said under his breath as Ray and his brother chased after Hardwick.

It certainly made the man look guilty.

Ray shouldered his way through the crowded bar, keeping his eyes on Hardwick as the ranch hand pushed his way to the front door. Brett darted the opposite direction hoping to cut Hardwick off before he reached the exit.

A brunette in a low-cut blouse touched his arm. "Buy you a drink, cowboy?"

Ray shook his head and forged on, catching glimpses of two other women attempting to snag Brett's attention. Although Brett had been a flirt and had had women galore when he was on the circuit, he barely noticed these ladies. He was completely devoted to Willow.

Ray spotted Hardwick elbow a couple aside in his haste to escape, then he darted out the door.

Ray rushed by the bar and made it to the exit before Brett, but Brett caught up quickly as they ran outside.

Ray paused to scan the parking lot, the music still blaring behind them, this time the song about a man and his dog.

"There, he's getting in his truck." Brett gestured at a black pickup and a custom tag that read "BIGMAN". Hardwick wrenched the door open and jumped in.

"Stop, Hardwick!" Ray shouted as he jogged through the parking lot.

By the time he reached Hardwick's truck, Hardwick was screeching from the parking lot.

Ray grabbed his keys from his pocket and motioned to Brett. "Come on, we'll take my Range Rover."

The two of them jogged to his SUV and got in. He fired up the engine and roared from the parking lot in chase. Tires squealed as Hardwick sped up and veered onto a side road.

A little sedan pulled out in front of Ray. He cursed and slowed, irritated that another car was coming toward him, and he couldn't pass it.

"Up there!" Brett pointed to the truck.

"I see it." Finally the oncoming car zoomed by, then another. Ray sped up and zoomed around the sedan. Accelerating, he rode the edge of the road until he made the turn.

Hardwick raced around a curve ahead. Ray

punched the gas and the Range Rover lurched forward, eating the distance between them.

Hardwick took a turn too fast and an oncoming gas truck appeared out of nowhere. Hardwick swerved to avoid it, but lost control and his truck left the road, flying toward a ravine.

Hardwick swung the truck to the right to avoid careening over the edge and diving into the hollow, but the truck spun out, then flipped to its side and skidded into an embankment. Glass shattered and metal crunched, sparks flying as it finally crashed to a stop.

"I'll call it in," Brett said as he reached for his phone.

Ray slowed the Range Rover and pulled onto the shoulder of the road, then jumped out and sprinted toward the vehicle.

It was upside down, the passenger side crunched against the embankment. He dropped down to his knees to look inside. The air bag had deployed and Hardwick was strapped in, upside down, and blood dripped down his face.

His eyes were closed and he wasn't moving.

"The ambulance is on its way," Brett said as he ran up. "How is he?"

"Hard to tell," Ray said. "He's unconscious."

Ray reached through the broken glass and felt for a pulse. "He's alive, but pulse is weak."

A siren wailed in the distance, indicating help

was on its way. Hardwick groaned and tried to open his eyes.

If he died, they'd never get any answers. "Why did you run, Hardwick?"

Another moan, and the man turned his head toward Ray.

"Did you set the fire at the barns on the ranch?" Brett asked.

Hardwick moved his head as if to shake it no, but it was difficult to tell. A siren wailed and the ambulance careened down the road toward them.

"Tell us," Brett said. "Did you set the fire?"

"No," Hardwick mumbled.

"You were working for Bennett?"

Hardwick coughed up blood, then faded into unconsciousness again. The ambulance roared to a stop, a fire engine on its tail.

Ray and Brett stepped aside as the rescue workers hurried toward them.

He didn't know if Hardwick would make it or not. But if he regained consciousness, they'd force him to talk.

SCARLET RUBBED HER ARMS, wondering where Ray was.

"I'll make sure the restraining order is in place and that Pullman knows about it," Deputy Whitefeather said. "Ray said he asked him about cutting the brake lines but he denied it."

"I wouldn't expect him to confess."

"If he did it, Scarlet, we'll find some way to get him."

"Thanks," Scarlet said. "I didn't want it to come to this."

Deputy Whitefeather gave her a sympathetic look. "It's not your fault. From what you've told me about the man, it sounds as if he has a pattern of abuse. He needs serious counseling and anger management classes."

"He also needs to stop drinking," Scarlet said. "I told him all this, but it only made him more furious."

"Sometimes it takes the court and a little jail time to knock some sense into people."

Even then it might not work. "The sad thing is that his child suffers. That little girl needs a father."

"Every kid does," the deputy said in a gravelly voice.

Scarlet didn't know the deputy very well, but she sensed they might be kindred spirits.

"Your father wasn't around?"

He shook his head, his long ponytail sliding over one shoulder. "No, I grew up on the reservation with my mother. I didn't even know my father's name until recently."

"I'm sorry," Scarlet said softly. "It sounds like you and I have some things in common."

The deputy's eyes darkened and, for a moment,

she thought she detected some strong emotions pass through them. Pain. Anger.

He was a handsome man. Big-boned, tall, tan skin, high cheekbones, eyes dark brown and soulful. Sexy.

But he didn't stir the same kind of need inside her that Ray McCullen did.

He heaved a breath and stood. "You know the McCullen brothers?"

Scarlet twisted her hands together, not sure how to answer that question. "I just met Ray. But I knew their father, Joe."

Deputy Whitefeather's brows rose in question. "You knew Joe McCullen?"

"Yes." Scarlet thought of Joe and had to smile. "I lived in the children's home outside Laramie. Joe volunteered there. He also donated money to build a new house. We named it The Family Farm."

"Really? That was nice of him."

"He had a soft spot for kids without families." Scarlet debated how much to tell him, but chose her words carefully. "He brought horses over twice a month and gave us riding lessons. I guess you could say he became a father figure to everyone there."

The deputy's jaw twitched. "I never knew the man myself, but I heard good things about him. Maddox took his death hard."

"I guess he was closest to Joe," Scarlet said.

"Yeah, I guess so." He narrowed his eyes at her. "You must have been upset, too."

Scarlet's chest ached with grief. "Yes, I loved him. He actually helped place me in another home when I was around ten. He…was always there for me." It made her sad to think she'd never see him again.

With all the trouble that had happened this week, he would have been the first person she would have called.

Now she'd called on his son Ray…

But that had to end. When his brothers discovered the truth about Barbara and Bobby and her, the McCullens probably wouldn't want them in their lives.

The deputy's dark gaze met hers, and once again, Scarlet had the uncanny sense that he wanted to say more. Turmoil colored his expression, one she didn't quite understand.

"Here's my card, Scarlet. Don't hesitate to call if you need anything."

"Thanks, Deputy Whitefeather. By the way, did Ray tell you that someone ran him off the road and beat him up?"

"Yes." His demeanor changed, suspicions flaring in his eyes. "It does seem like someone's out to get the McCullens."

He couldn't possibly think she'd hurt Ray or the McCullens. But Bobby might… "I hope you find whoever did it. It could be the same person who set that fire."

The deputy squeezed her arm. "Don't worry, Scarlet, we'll get to the bottom of this. Just keep your doors locked and call me if Pullman shows up again."

She locked the door when he left and prayed no one else came to her house tonight. Not Pullman or Bobby.

Or Ray.

If he returned, she wouldn't be able to resist asking him to stay.

IT TOOK FOREVER for the firefighters to extract Hardwick from his truck, board him and transport him to the hospital.

The medics said he had a concussion, cuts and abrasions, and they were worried about internal bleeding.

Ray drove Brett to retrieve his truck at The Silver Bullet, then they met at the hospital. If Hardwick regained consciousness, they wanted to be there to question him.

Ray went straight to the coffee machine while Brett called Willow to check on her and Sam.

Ray brought his brother a cup of coffee and sipped his own. It was weak but warmed his throat, and after being up most of the night he needed the jolt of caffeine.

Brett removed his Stetson and raked his hand through his hair. "Thanks, man."

"Look, Brett, we may be here for hours. Why don't you go on home to Willow and Sam?" A twinge of jealousy niggled at Ray. Brett and Maddox both had families now, women who loved and cared about them.

Nobody gave a damn about him.

He'd always liked it that way. But Scarlet's face flashed in his mind—an image of her nearly naked, her cheeks flushed with passion—and he had an urge to go back to her tonight.

Brett glanced up at him, a sheepish look on his face. "I do miss them, but I don't want to let you or Maddox down, Ray. Finding out who set fire to those barns is important. They might try again."

Ray's gut tightened, feeling more connected to his brothers than he had in years. "You're right. If they attack the ranch, they attack us. All the more reason you should go home to your wife and son," he continued. "They need you. And someone should be on the ranch in case something else happens."

"I left Clyde in charge."

"I know he cares about Horseshoe Creek," Ray said. "But not like we do."

A grin tugged at Brett's face. "That mean you're not going to sell out and leave?"

"I'm not selling," Ray said emphatically. Although he didn't know if he'd stick around. Coming back home to Pistol Whip had triggered the sense of betrayal he'd felt at his father's affair.

It had also stirred good memories of carousing with his brothers when he was small. Of riding across the ranch, working with his hands and living off the land.

Not that he'd give up his PI business. He liked his work. But he could do that here…

He gritted his teeth. Was he really thinking about moving back?

"Seriously, Brett, go home. I'll call you if Hardwick wakes up and I talk to him."

Brett looked reluctant, but finally agreed. "Thanks, man."

Ray nodded, grateful Brett would be at the ranch tonight in case more trouble arose. If Bennett had hired Hardwick or someone else to set the fire, he could have others working for him.

Just as Brett left, his phone buzzed. Deputy Whitefeather. "Yeah?"

"I talked to Scarlet. She's safe now. I'll take care of the restraining order."

"Thanks. Any word on the DNA from that cigarette?"

"Not yet. I'll call the lab and ask them to hurry it up."

"Thanks. I'm at the hospital. We got a lead from one of our hands about a worker named Hardwick. Brett and I tracked him to The Silver Bullet but he ran. We chased him in our car, but he crashed. He's in the ER now."

"You want me to meet you there?"

"No, just find out what you can on Hardwick. If we can trace financials between Bennett and him, or if Hardwick has a record, we could use it to force him to talk."

"I'm on it, but so far on paper Bennett looks legit."

"Keep at it."

"I will." The deputy hesitated. "Call me if you remember anything else about the man who attacked you."

Ray agreed, and the deputy ended the call. Ray sipped his coffee and paced while he waited on the doctor to let him speak to Hardwick.

A half hour later, the nurse finally relayed the news that Hardwick was going to make it, and that he was awake.

Ray followed her to the ER cube, his body tense as he approached the man. Hardwick was battered and bruised, a bandage around his head, one arm in a sling. His eyes looked bleary as he followed Ray's approach.

"Looks like you're going to make it, Hardwick. I talked to the deputy. He'll transport you to jail as soon as you're released."

Hardwick's eyes widened in fear. "What the hell for? I haven't done anything."

"It was your cigarette butt in the barn, wasn't it? Did Bennett pay you to set the barn on fire?"

Hardwick coughed, his voice weak. "No, just to report back what you were doing."

Ray heaved a breath. So he admitted being at the barn. "I don't believe you," Ray said. "I think he wanted you to sabotage our place and that he has more plans, maybe something bigger."

Hardwick broke into another coughing fit, the machine beeping that his blood pressure was dropping.

The nurse rushed in with a scowl. "You'll have to go, sir."

Ray leaned closer to Hardwick. "If you didn't do it, give me a name."

Hardwick coughed again, struggling with each breath, and the nurse grabbed Ray's arm. "I said you need to leave."

Ray held firm and growled in Hardwick's ear. "Tell me, dammit."

"Romley," Hardwick choked out. "Talk to him."

Ray nodded, yanked away from the nurse and strode to the door. Romley was the hand he'd seen smoking with Hardwick.

He hurried to his Range Rover, then started the engine and drove back toward Horseshoe Creek.

His phone buzzed and he checked it. Brett. He punched Connect. "Yeah."

"Did Hardwick talk?"

"He said he didn't set the fire, but he was spying on our progress. He also told me to talk to Romley. I'm on my way back. I'll swing by his bunkhouse."

"All right. But listen, Ray. Maddox just called and said he and Rose will be home late tonight. He wants to talk to us first thing in the morning. Something about the will."

Ray's pulse jumped. "Did he say anything else?"

"No, but he insisted we both needed to be there." Brett hesitated. "I think something's wrong."

Dread balled in Ray's stomach. He felt as if a time bomb had started ticking inside his head.

Had Maddox discovered their father's dirty little secret?

Chapter Sixteen

Tension knotted every muscle in Ray's body as he drove back to Horseshoe Creek. Long ago, his father had built cabins on the property for the cook, the head horse trainer and groomer, and for the foreman and his family. He'd also built bunkhouses for ranch hands, especially those who took seasonal jobs.

Ten minutes later, he bypassed the cabin where Brett, Willow and Sam were living, noting the lights were off, so they must have turned in for the night. He scanned the ranch land as he drove, looking for trouble and praying he didn't find it.

That whoever had set that fire wouldn't return. But he couldn't count on that.

Brett had been working day and night overseeing the additions to the ranch, buying and bringing in more horses, and supervising the building of his home with Willow. The sprawling farmhouse was set on a hill by the creek surrounded by giant trees and pastureland with a view of the sunset that could be seen from the front porch. Brett had also built his own barn to keep horses for his family to ride for leisure.

Ray envisioned himself riding across the ranch with a woman and maybe a kid, and his mouth grew dry. Could he ever see himself settling down with a family?

Scarlet's face taunted him, and he nearly ran into a ditch. He blinked and yanked the Range Rover onto the road, then turned down the drive leading to the bunkhouses. The lights were off in most of them, as well. Ranch hands started at daylight and went to bed at dark.

Hardwick and Romley lived in the one on the end, and he slowed as he approached. His gaze swept the pasture behind and surrounding the bunkhouse, but didn't see movement.

Hoping to catch Romley off guard, Ray slowed his vehicle and parked at the first bunkhouse. He eased open the door and slid from the interior, tucking his gun inside his jacket as he walked. Gravel crunched beneath his boots, and the wind nearly ripped off his hat, but he jammed it firmly on his head and strode forward.

When he reached the bunkhouse, he realized there was only one truck parked by it. Was it Romley's?

He squared his shoulders, climbed the two steps

to the stoop, then raised his fist and knocked. Once, twice. He paused to listen for sounds inside.

A light flicked on, and footsteps sounded inside. Ray braced himself for a confrontation as the door opened. A rail-thin young man in his early twenties stood on the other side, scratching his head, his hair sticking up. Not Romley.

"What's your name, man?" Ray asked.

"Curtis."

"Ray McCullen." Ray gestured inside. "I'm looking for Stan Romley."

"He's not here. Left out earlier."

"What do you mean, he left out?" Ray shouldered his way inside, flipped on an overhead light and surveyed the interior of the cabin. A main living area/kitchen and two rooms on each side, both rooms housed with bunks.

One bed was unmade. Curtis's. He'd obviously been sleeping. The rest of the beds were turned up, although a duffel bag, shoes and personal items filled one corner in the room opposite Curtis's.

Ray examined the clothes and bag. "Whose is this?"

"Hardwick's. It was just the three of us in here, but Romley came in about five o'clock, grabbed his stuff and rushed out."

Had Hardwick tipped him off that they were on to them?

"Did he mention where he was going?"

Curtis shook his head. "I asked him if he was

coming back and he said no. I figured something must have happened and you all laid him off."

Ray silently cursed.

He checked the desk drawer in the corner, then Hardwick's duffel bag in search of a hint as to what the two men had planned.

That turned up nothing.

"Did he do something wrong?" Curtis asked.

Ray slanted the young man a curious look. "I think he and Hardwick set the fire that destroyed our new barns." He watched Curtis for a reaction. "Do you know anything about that?"

The young man took a step back, his lips thinning. "No. Hell, no."

"You help them?"

Curtis held up his hands in a defensive gesture. "Listen, Mr. McCullen, I just got this job last week. I only met Hardwick and Romley when I came on board."

"How about Arlis Bennett? Do you know him?"

"I've heard his name, everyone around Pistol Whip has," Curtis said.

"Have you ever worked for him?"

"No." Curtis's voice cracked. "I swear, Mr. McCullen, I wouldn't do anything against you and your brothers. I was hired on 'cause I'm a fan of Brett's, and I was hoping he could teach me some riding tricks."

Ray relaxed slightly. He could hear the hero

worship in the young man's voice. And God knows, Brett had fans.

"Did you ever hear Hardwick or Romley talking about Bennett? Or about sabotaging our operation?"

"No," Curtis said. "But last night Hardwick said they needed to finish here and get out of town. I thought they had another job lined up."

They did, Ray thought with a grimace. A big paycheck, probably from Bennett.

SCARLET TOSSED AND turned all night. She kept listening for sounds of an intruder, afraid Bobby or Pullman would return.

Tomorrow at noon they would meet with the lawyer to hear the reading of the will.

As excited as she'd been over Joe's donation to The Family Farm, she was equally anxious about Ray's brothers' reactions.

She closed her eyes but shivered as she thought about Bobby—whatever stipulation Joe had put on his share, Bobby wouldn't like it.

Ray's sexy face materialized, replacing Bobby's antagonistic one, stirring feelings she couldn't allow herself to feel... Would she see him again after the reading?

A noise sounded outside, and she rolled over and listened. Wind, rain, the windowpanes rattling. The noises went on and on, keeping her nerves on edge.

Finally at dawn, she gave up on sleep, punched the pillow, got up and showered. A faint stream of sunlight wormed its way through the bleak-looking sky, the gray cast mirroring her mood.

She faced herself in the mirror and gave herself a pep talk. Joe had included her because he knew she'd use her inheritance to help needy children. If the McCullens questioned her intentions, she'd find a way to convince them how much he'd cared about The Family Farm.

She dressed, taking more time with her makeup than usual to camouflage the bruises from her accident and the dark circles beneath her eyes due to lack of sleep.

Despite her nerves, she managed to eat some toast and sipped her coffee while she finished the paperwork for the Fullers' adoption. Then she drove to The Family Farm and spent the morning with the smaller children who didn't yet attend school.

As she left, Corey hugged her, and her heart warmed. One day she wanted a family of her own.

For now though these kids were her family just like Joe had been. It didn't matter if they were blood related. She loved them just the same.

And she would do everything she could to make sure they were taken care of.

RAY'S STOMACH WAS in knots as he entered his father's office. Mama Mary had set coffee in the office along with breakfast, but he couldn't eat until he talked to his brothers.

Maddox was waiting, a steaming mug in his hand, and Brett loped in a second later.

"I thought we'd better conference before the reading," Maddox said.

"Something wrong?" Brett asked as he poured his own coffee.

"I got a heads-up from Dad's lawyer that there were some complications to the will. He wouldn't elaborate, though."

Ray cleared his throat, irritated that Bush hadn't returned his call. He couldn't avoid the dreaded conversation any longer. "I planned to talk to you guys when you got back, Maddox."

Maddox arched his brows. "You know what this is about?"

Ray nodded. "You'd both better sit down."

Brett scowled. "What's going on?"

A muscle jumped in Maddox's jaw. "I don't like the sound of this."

He wasn't going to like anything about it, but Ray couldn't keep his father's secret any longer.

"There's something I need to say, and I want you both to just listen. It's about Dad."

Both his brothers looked confused.

"If you want to sell your share, just let us know," Maddox said.

"It's not that," Ray said. "It's the reason Dad and I didn't get along."

Brett ran a hand through his hair. "Ray, that's water under the bridge. We all had our differences."

"You don't understand," Ray said. "Just listen."

Brett started to smart off, but Maddox gestured to let Ray speak.

Ray took a deep breath and began. "Dad had an affair before Mom died. The woman's name was Barbara."

Brett looked shocked. Maddox did as well, although something else flared in his eyes. Recognition.

"You knew?" Ray asked him.

Maddox gave a short shake of his head. "No. At least not about the affair. I knew he dated a woman named Barbara later on, when we were teenagers."

"How did you know about it, Ray?" Brett asked.

The image of his father in bed with that woman taunted Brett. "I walked in on them one day. In bed. I was five."

"That's the reason you were always so mad at Dad," Maddox said matter-of-factly.

Ray nodded.

"Why didn't you ever tell us?" Brett asked.

"I didn't really understand what was going on, but I promised Dad I wouldn't tell. Later on, he claimed he broke it off with her, said he was sorry, that he loved Mom. He said he didn't want to hurt her so it would be our secret." He bit out the words. "I knew it was wrong, but I didn't want to hurt her."

Maddox crossed his arms. "So you didn't tell us, either."

"He didn't want you to know," Ray said, remembering the turmoil he'd felt. "You looked up to him. I didn't want to mess that up."

A tense silence ensued while his brothers processed the information. Maddox pinched the bridge of his nose, his face strained.

"I always thought Dad had a wandering eye," Brett admitted.

"He said Mom forgave him before she died," Ray said. "That's why he wanted to see me before he passed."

"I don't know what to say," Maddox muttered. "I'm sorry, Ray. You shouldn't have had to carry that burden all these years."

Another heartbeat passed. "There's more."

Brett pulled a hand down his chin. "What more can there be?"

"Dad and Barbara had a child. A boy named Bobby. He's about my age."

Maddox cursed and Brett dropped his head into his hands.

"That's what Bush was talking about, isn't it?" Maddox asked.

Ray nodded. "I'm afraid so."

Brett lifted his head, anger glittering in his eyes. "You knew about the kid, too?"

"Not until a couple of days ago," Ray said.

"Where is he?" Brett asked.

"He grew up living with Barbara not too far away."

Maddox cursed again. "This is unbelievable."

Brett jumped up and paced the room. "Dad should have told us."

"This guy Bobby? He wants part of Horseshoe Creek?" Maddox growled.

"I think so." Ray paused. "When I found out—"

Brett whirled on him. "How did you find out?"

"It's a long story," Ray began.

"Tell us everything," Maddox said in a tone that brooked no argument. "We have to know what we're up against before we walk into the lawyer's office today."

Maddox was right. Ray got more coffee and so did his brothers, and they gathered around the fireplace.

Both his brothers sat rigid as he explained about Scarlet's visit, The Family Farm and how she'd come to live with Barbara and Bobby.

"Apparently Bobby resented Scarlet. He hated us and her for the attention Dad gave us," Ray finished.

"So Bobby may want revenge against us." Brett paused, mind working. "Why didn't you tell me this before? He could have set the fire."

"I know that," Ray said. "I've been investigating him myself. Barbara claims he was with her that night."

"You met Barbara?" Maddox asked.

Ray nodded on a pained sigh. "I had to. I wanted to find out if either of them had anything to do with the fire."

"Let me guess—they alibied each other," Maddox said in a derisive tone. "Perfect cover."

"Hell, they could have been in on it together," Brett snapped.

"I'm aware of that." Ray braced his elbows on his knees.

"You're sure Dad included Barbara and this girl, Scarlet, in the will?" Maddox asked in an incredulous voice.

"Yeah. According to the letter Scarlet received. They'll probably be at the reading today. Although it doesn't make sense that they'd set the fire before finding out what Dad left them."

"What did he leave them?" Brett asked.

"I don't know. I called Bush and asked him to phone me back, but he never did."

"I can't believe Dad did this to us," Brett said bitterly. "What are we going to do?"

Maddox set his mug down with a thud. "I know one thing we're not going to do. Give in to them. They're not getting Horseshoe Creek. It belongs to us."

SCARLET SWALLOWED BACK nausea as she drove to the lawyer's office. Had Ray warned his brothers about her and Barbara and Bobby?

When she arrived, she spotted Ray's Range Rover along with the sheriff's SUV. Maddox had probably driven it to intentionally intimidate them.

She hoped Bobby behaved and Maddox didn't have to use his badge against him. Joe would have hated that.

Trembling with nerves, she parked, then closed her eyes for a moment, picturing Joe laughing with the kids at The Family Farm as he'd taught them how to mount a horse. The first time he'd helped her up, she'd fallen in love with the quiet-tempered palomino.

She'd wanted a horse of her own.

But that hadn't happened. He had given her a home, though. And for a little while, she'd thought Barbara loved her.

It didn't matter. She'd survived. She would get through today, take whatever Joe had offered and use it in his honor.

Her mouth was so dry, she dabbed lip-gloss on her lips, smoothed down the sweater she'd chosen to wear with her denim skirt and climbed out. Her boot heel caught on one of the stones in the parking lot, but she managed to stay on her feet until she reached the door of the office.

A bell tinkled when she entered, alerting the

receptionist at the desk facing the doorway. The middle-aged woman rose and smiled at her.

"Miss Lovett?"

"Yes."

"Mr. Bush and the McCullens are waiting in Mr. Bush's office."

She gathered her courage and followed the woman into the office. The lawyer sat in a leather wing chair in the center while Maddox, Brett and Ray occupied chairs lined on one wall. A heavy-set woman with short curly hair sat by the men, her hands knotted around her purse. Scarlet recognized her from Joe's description—she was Mama Mary, the cook and housekeeper who'd been part of the family for years.

Three other chairs were situated on the opposite one.

If she hadn't been so anxious, she would have laughed. The lines had obviously been drawn.

The three McCullen men stood and faced her, all handsome as sin.

But the looks they were giving her were definitely wary. Not friendly. Antagonistic even.

Mama Mary's expression seemed more neutral, although she fidgeted as if she was nervous.

Ray's gaze met hers, and her stomach fluttered with that unrelenting need to be close to him.

"This is her?" Maddox asked.

Ray nodded, his expression unreadable. "Yes, Maddox, Brett, Mama Mary, this is Scarlet Lovett, the young lady Dad took under his wing at The Family Farm."

Tension stretched between them, riddled with unanswered questions and distrust.

Before she could speak, a noise reverberated from the outer room, then Bobby strode in, looking smug and raring for a fight. Barbara was right behind him, her hand on his arm, obviously terrified that Bobby was going to act out.

Judging from the fierce look in the McCullen men's eyes, they were prepared for battle, as well.

Chapter Seventeen

Ray struggled with mixed emotions as Scarlet slid into a seat. She looked small and uneasy, but she lifted her chin as if she didn't intend to let his brothers or the Lowmans intimidate her.

The lawyer cleared his throat. "Now that everyone is here, let's take a seat."

"Don't you think we should introduce ourselves?" Maddox asked.

Bush's face blanched. "I'm sorry, of course." Bush stood behind his desk. "I'm Darren Bush, Joe McCullen's attorney. While I've met you, Maddox, Brett, Ray and Mama Mary, I have not met Bobby and Barbara Lowman." He extended his hand in a friendly overture.

Bobby shook his hand but gave Ray and his brothers a cutting look. "You must be Barbara?" Bush asked.

She fluffed her dark bob with one hand, then

shook Bush's proffered one. "Yes. It's nice to meet you, Mr. Bush."

She pivoted to face Maddox and Brett. "I understand that you may not feel this way, but I am glad to finally meet you boys. Your father adored all of you."

"He talked about us with you?" Maddox asked.

Barbara nodded. "Of course, I realize this is awkward and that finding out about me came as a shock to you, Maddox, and to you, Brett."

"Yes, it did," Brett said. "I still can't figure out the reason he never came clean."

Bobby stepped forward, his expression defensive. "You make it sound like it was my fault."

Brett squared his shoulders. "That's not what I meant."

Scarlet cleared her throat. "Joe kept his families separate because he didn't want to hurt anyone."

Maddox pivoted toward Scarlet. "You knew about us?"

"Yes. But not until a couple of years ago." Scarlet twined her fingers together. "After Joe got sick, he broke down and told me while we were riding one day. He said he wanted to make things right."

Ray turned to Bobby. "When did you learn about us?"

Bobby glared at his mother. "When I was a teenager. But not because Dad told me. I heard him and Mom arguing one night."

Ray jammed his hands in the pockets of his jeans. "Did you confront him?"

Bobby pulled at his chin. "Damn right I did. But he tried to justify keeping me away from you guys by saying he'd take care of me and Mom."

Bobby started to say something else, but Barbara caught his arm. "And he's going to, Bobby. I told you he loved you and he did." She motioned for him to sit down. "Maddox, Brett, Ray. I loved your father very much. He and I never meant to hurt you with our relationship. That's also the reason Bobby never tried to contact you. We both respected your father and his life with you."

Barbara sounded sincere, but Bobby's jaw twitched with resentment as if he didn't share that sentiment.

Scarlet's comment about Barbara echoed in Ray's head—in the beginning, Scarlet thought Barbara loved her. Later she realized the woman had only given her a home to appease their father.

Bush rapped his knuckles on the desk. "All right, now that we've made the introductions, let's sit down and get to it." He gave them all a stern look. "Let me remind you that this will was issued and signed by Joe McCullen, that the contents were his wishes. I spoke with him and witnessed the signing. Also, if there is any problem or if you want to contest any part of it, you must go through legal channels. I do not expect an altercation in here. I expect professional, mature conduct from everyone."

"Of course," Maddox said.

Bush glanced at each of them in turn, and they all agreed. Then everyone seated themselves, and Bush opened the document and began to read his father's last will and testament.

SCARLET SAT IN stunned silence in a corner all on her own while the lawyer read the will. Most of it was as she'd expected. Maddox, the oldest brother, was the executor.

He and Brett and Ray inherited the ranch along with Joe's assets, which included a hefty life insurance policy, their portion to be divided equally three ways. If one of them chose to sell his or her share of the ranch, they were required to sell to the other McCullens so the ranch would remain McCullen land.

He'd also made provisions for Mama Mary, ensuring her salary, a savings account and that she would remain part of the ranch family as long as she lived. Joe had also purchased an insurance policy in her name to take care of her if she became ill.

Mama Mary dabbed at her eyes as Ray squeezed her hand.

"Of course she'll stay," Maddox said.

Brett rose and hugged the woman. "You're our mama, you're family."

She hugged each of them, wiping at tears. Bush paused to allow her to regain control, then continued, "In addition, Joe had a secondary life insurance policy valued at two hundred and fifty thousand dollars, which is to be divided among Barbara and Bobby Lowman and Scarlet Lovett," Bush said.

Surprised looks floated around the room.

"Miss Lovett, Joe explained that you were the daughter to him that he never had. He admired your dedication and hard work with the children at The Family Farm, and for your personal use, he left you a sum total of fifty thousand dollars."

Scarlet inhaled, well aware that Bobby was seething as he sat ramrod straight beside Barbara. "In addition, he left you ten acres at the south end of Horseshoe Creek, land which already holds a cabin where you may live if you choose."

Maddox, Brett and Ray exchanged a look, but said nothing. After all, what was ten acres when they owned several hundred?

"In addition, he donated a hundred thousand dollars of his life insurance to The Family Farm. That money and its use are to be supervised and managed by you."

Scarlet smiled, grateful that Joe had been generous with The Family Farm. She intended to pay it forward just as Joe had done with her.

"I'd be honored," she said, then bit her tongue when the room fell into an awkward silence.

Mr. Bush shifted in his seat, obviously uncomfortable. "For the last section of the will, Barbara Lowman, Joe McCullen paid off the house you live in and left you a sum of fifty thousand dollars for your personal use."

Barbara's sharp intake reeked of disappointment.

"And last, Bobby Lowman, Joe McCullen named you as his fourth son. You shall receive a lump sum of fifty thousand dollars along with a share of Horseshoe Creek, a section of seventy-five acres at the north end of the ranch that he recently purchased for you.

Bush addressed Bobby. "However, Joe placed stipulations on ownership of the property."

Bobby lurched up, eyes glinting. "What the hell?"

"What are the stipulations?" Barbara asked.

Bush directed his comments toward Bobby again. "Mr. McCullen stipulated that in order to receive your share of the life insurance policy and the property, you enter into a rehab program and receive counseling."

"What?" Bobby said in a seething tone.

"Sit down, son." Barbara took his arm to keep him from bolting—or attacking someone.

"There's one more stipulation," Bush continued. "While you do own the land he willed to you, if you choose to sell, you must sell to the McCullens. If you decide to keep the property and reside on it, you must work the land. Maddox will supervise and consult with you to help you set up a working operation so that you can make a profit and earn enough to live off."

RAY STARED AT the lawyer in shock. He felt the same unsettled surprise radiating from his brothers. Maddox looked as if he could shoot someone.

Bobby made a low menacing sound in his throat. "This is ridiculous," Bobby snapped.

"I'm sorry you feel that way," Bush said. "But these were Joe's wishes. If you want your inheritance, you are required by law to comply with the guidelines he established."

Barbara rubbed Bobby's back. "Come on, son. This is a lot to absorb. Let's get some lunch and talk."

Maddox stood and started to say something, but Barbara threw up a warning hand. "Not right now. We need some time."

The hurt lacing her voice tugged at Ray. As much as he resented what his father had done to them with his lies and betrayal, and as much as he wanted to protect Horseshoe Creek, he understood Bobby's anger and resentment. The last thing their half brother probably wanted was to be watched by one of Joe's sons and have to earn his approval.

How had their father expected Maddox or any of them to work together?

Bobby stalked from the room, Barbara behind him. The door slammed shut in their wake, leaving a mountain of tension lingering.

Scarlet glanced at Ray as if asking what she should do, but he had no answers. While he'd had a couple of days to accept her part in his father's life, Maddox and Brett had just learned about her and the Lowmans.

Disappointment flickered in Scarlet's eyes, then she rose, brushing at her skirt. "Thank you, Mr. Bush."

"If you'll leave your banking information with my secretary," Bush said, "I'll make sure the check is deposited directly into your account. As far as The Family Farm goes, the money for them will go into a business account to be used at your discretion for their needs."

"Of course," Scarlet said. "I work closely with the director. She and I are thrilled to honor Joe in this way."

Bush shook her hand. "Joe must have trusted you a great deal."

Scarlet glanced at Ray and his brothers, but the men remained silent.

"He knows how much the children and that place mean to me," Scarlet said. "It was my home for a lot of years. I intend to do right by those children, just like Joe did by me."

Bush nodded. "About the cabin and land—"

"We'll work that out later," Scarlet said. "I'm fine in my rental house for now."

Clutching her purse to her, she disappeared out the door.

Maddox folded his arms and began to grill the lawyer, but Ray ducked through the door after Scarlet.

He found her outside the office, her arms wrapped around her waist as she took deep breaths. She looked shaken and small and vulnerable.

Why had his father handled things this way? He'd left a damn mess.

He eased up behind her, struggling with what to say. "Scarlet, are you okay?"

She spun around, her lower lip quivering. "I'm fine, Ray. I loved Joe and miss him. And for the record, I never expected anything from him. You have to believe that."

He did believe her. "He wanted you to have it, though. He obviously loved you and that children's home."

Ray lifted his hand and stroked her cheek with the pad of his thumb. "Maddox and Brett just need time to process this."

Scarlet offered him a tentative smile. "I understand. I'm sorry."

Damn, she looked like an angel. "It's not your fault," Ray said. "My father made this mess." But they had to clean it up. And that wasn't going to be easy, not with Bobby's attitude.

"It is complicated," Scarlet said. "Joe wasn't perfect. He didn't tell you all the truth because he didn't want to disappoint you."

Ray's chest constricted. He'd done that a long time ago.

But still, Joe was his father and he loved him.

"Do you plan to move into the cabin?" Ray asked.

"Yes, *do* you?" Maddox asked.

Scarlet's breath quickened at the sound of Maddox's gruff tone. Ray dropped his hand from her cheek and turned to face his oldest brother. He'd never felt as if he could live up to Maddox.

"I don't know, but like I said, I'm in no hurry." Scarlet tilted her chin upward. "But I will use the funds he designated for The Family Farm for the good of the children. You're all invited to visit it and meet the children anytime you want. I think you'd be proud of what your father accomplished there."

"You certainly seem to know a lot about our father," Maddox said.

Scarlet flinched. "He was an important influence in my life for over ten years. I won't forget that."

"Why you?" Brett asked. "Why did he take you in?"

Scarlet's voice softened. "Joe saw how I grew up and knew he could let down his guard with me. You guys held him to a higher standard. He wanted to be your hero."

Maddox looked down at his boots, his face strained. Joe had been his hero. Until now.

Brett shifted and looked away, too, but he seemed to be contemplating her statement.

"Like I said, let me know if you want to come by The Family Farm." Scarlet clenched her purse with one hand, walked down the steps to her car and got inside. Ray wanted to follow her and make sure she was okay.

Hell, he wanted to hold her and kiss her and love her through the day and night.

But Maddox and Brett were waiting, and they had to talk.

"Was she sleeping with Dad?" Brett asked.

Ray's temper flared, and he spun around to face his brothers. "No. I investigated her when she first came to me. The director at the children's home assured me that she's legit. Joe thought of her as the daughter he never had."

Maddox scowled. "Maybe Dad wasn't sleeping with her, but you are, aren't you, Ray?" He glared at him. "You knew who she was, and that she and that woman and her son wanted part of Dad's ranch, but you jumped into bed with her anyway, didn't you?"

SCARLET MENTALLY SHOOK off her anxiety over the confrontation between Bobby and Ray and his brothers as she drove to The Family Farm. All in all, the meeting had gone better than she expected. At least Bobby hadn't started throwing punches.

But he was upset. There was no doubt about that.

Although Joe was right—Bobby needed rehab and counseling. If he committed to that, maybe he'd realize that Joe had given him an opportunity for a future. And perhaps one day a relationship with his half brothers.

She parked and rushed inside the children's home, then found Millie in the kitchen baking cinnamon rolls. The kids were in school now, the ones too young for school outside in the play yard.

Two volunteers watched the little ones while Faye was in the office on the computer.

She poked her head in. "Faye, I just came from the will reading."

"How did it go?" Faye asked.

"Good." Scarlet smiled. "He left a hundred thousand dollars to the home. I'm supposed to oversee how we use it. I plan to talk to a financial advisor about an investment plan so the money can keep working for us."

Faye blinked back tears. "That's wonderful, Scarlet. I knew Joe wouldn't let us down."

Maddox and Brett didn't exactly see his donation that way. And frankly, Ray hadn't exactly defended her in front of his family. If push came to shove, would he team up with them to contest her inheritance?

She pushed aside her worry and went to visit the children, then drove to her office for the afternoon.

Just as she was about to step inside, footsteps crunched behind her. She froze, but suddenly someone jerked her backward.

She tried to scream, but a cold, hard hand clamped down over her mouth, cutting her off. Then the man dragged her around the corner and pressed her face into the side of the building.

Chapter Eighteen

Ray clenched his jaw. "Why don't we discuss this at home?"

Maddox looked furious while Brett's expression was unreadable.

"He's right," Brett said.

"Fine." Maddox strode to his police vehicle and he and Brett followed him to the ranch in their own vehicles.

When they parked and went in, Mama Mary set her purse on the side table. "I'll get lunch."

"We'll eat later," Maddox said.

Mama Mary looked hurt. "I'm sorry, boys. I know today was difficult on you,"

"We'll work it out," Ray said, earning a contemptuous look from Maddox.

"Let's sit down in Dad's office," Brett suggested.

The four of them claimed seats around the coffee table in the sitting area.

Maddox took the lead and turned to Mama Mary. She wrung her hands together.

"You knew about Barbara and her son, didn't you?" Maddox asked.

Guilt streaked Mama Mary's face. "I knew about the woman, but not the boy. I...can't believe Mr. Joe left this world without explaining everything to you all."

"He was a coward," Ray said.

Maddox and Brett both nodded as if they agreed.

"Don't be too hard on your daddy," Mama Mary said. "He was just a man. None of you are perfect, either."

"I would never cheat on Rose," Maddox said.

Brett looked sheepish. "I know I was a player, but I'm committed to Willow now, and I would never hurt her by fooling around."

"It was a long time ago," Mama Mary said. "Besides, you don't know what caused him to stray. He and your mama...well, just like all couples, they had problems."

"What kind of problems?" Maddox asked.

"That's all I can say." Mama Mary tapped her foot up and down. "Just that there's always two sides to a story. Now your daddy is gone, try to remember the good times. How much he loved all of you. That he didn't tell you because he didn't want to upset you."

"Then why did he include his mistress and her son in his will?" Maddox asked.

Mama Mary gave Maddox a scolding look. "Because like it or not, they are family, Maddox. He had to do right by them, too. You best accept that fact."

Maddox's boots hit the floor and he paced to the window. "I may have to accept it, but I don't like it."

"I don't trust Barbara or Bobby," Brett added.

Ray cleared his throat. "We shouldn't trust him," Ray said. "He's been in trouble with the law before, and he can be violent. That's the reason Dad stipulated he needs to enter into rehab."

"How the hell am I supposed to help him set up his own spread?" Maddox said, his voice incredulous. "Didn't Dad realize what he was asking of both of us?"

"Yeah, even if we accept him," Brett said. "Bobby obviously resents us."

"And what about that girl Scarlet?" Maddox turned on Ray again. "What if she's in cahoots with Bobby? Who knows that they won't come back and ask for more?"

"She's not like that," Ray said.

Maddox's brows rose. "Good God. You *are* involved with her, aren't you?"

Just like always, Maddox's disapproval rang through loud and clear.

"No," Ray said, although a voice inside his head shouted, *Liar.*

Ray's phone buzzed and he checked the screen. Deputy Whitefeather.

"I have to answer this." He pressed Connect. "This is Ray."

"Deputy Whitefeather. Listen, Ray, a man named Hugh Weatherman phoned the office. He says he works with Scarlet Lovett and that he spotted Pullman near her office."

"What about that restraining order?"

"Pullman's obviously not concerned about it. Anyway, this man, Hugh, claims Scarlet was supposed to be at the office a half hour ago, but he hasn't seen her. Said her car is outside, but she's not. I thought she might be with you."

"No. Are you at her office now?"

"No, I had a lead on Romley. I'm twenty minutes outside town."

Ray silently cursed. "I'm on my way. Keep us posted if you find Romley."

Whitefeather agreed, and Ray yanked his keys from his pocket.

"What's going on?" Maddox asked as he ended the call and headed to the door.

"Scarlet had to remove a child from her home, and the father is out to get her. That was her co-worker. He's worried. Scarlet never showed at her office."

Maddox adjusted his weapon. "Where's her office?"

"I can handle this, Maddox," Ray said.

Maddox caught his arm. "I'm the sheriff. It's my job, Ray."

"Please, Maddox. I'll call you if I need you. Just stay here and figure out what to do about Bobby."

Ray rushed to the door. Right now he needed a break from his big brother, needed to find Scarlet and make sure she was all right without Maddox breathing down his neck.

But if that bastard had her, he'd call Maddox. That is, if he didn't kill Pullman himself.

SCARLET TWISTED SIDEWAYS to escape the man's grip, but he dragged her farther down the alley between the buildings. He pushed her into an overhang from the abandoned warehouse, then shoved her face-first against the wall, grinding her cheek into the brick.

"Who are you? What do you want?" she managed to choke out.

"Just shut up and listen, Scarlet."

Bobby. She should have known when she smelled whiskey on his breath. "This is crazy, Bobby. You should be happy. You just inherited some money and land."

"Happy?" Bobby hissed against her ear. "Dad left me nothing compared to what those McCullen boys got."

"He left you enough to start a new life." Scarlet closed her eyes, tired of Bobby's selfishness.

"Maybe he would have given you more if you'd been responsible."

He yanked her arm behind her back, making pain shoot up her shoulder. "He was the one who treated me badly. He was always at that damn ranch with his *real* kids. He was ashamed of me."

"No, he wasn't, Bobby. And it's not too late to make him proud," Scarlet said. "Take the land and build your own spread."

He shoved his knee against the back of her legs and she cried out in pain. "You didn't have to do anything to get your share."

"Yes, I did. I have a job helping those needy children. That's the reason Joe left me money. So take what he left you and be grateful."

"Yeah, take the leftover scraps just like I've always done."

"It's better than nothing," Scarlet said. "And if you go to rehab—"

"I don't need a damn bunch of people picking at my mind," Bobby rasped.

"But if you do that and work with Maddox, you can have your own ranch."

"I should have a fourth of Horseshoe Creek," he hissed. "How could Dad expect me to work under Maddox McCullen?"

Her mind raced with a way to defuse the situation. "Because Maddox is experienced and can teach you about ranching."

Bobby jerked her around and shoved her hands

above her head. "You're so damn naive," Bobby said bitterly. "The McCullens are probably plotting right now to get rid of me."

Scarlet struggled for a breath. Unfortunately he might be right. "Maybe you should talk to them instead of me."

"That's right, you're not family at all. But you still received the same amount of money as me. Even more if you count the money for that damned orphanage."

A sinister gleam glittered in Bobby's eyes, and she realized where he was headed with this talk.

"You want the money Joe designated for those children?"

Bobby nodded. "It should be mine. I was his son."

"Don't be greedy," Scarlet said in a throaty whisper. "You know how much helping those children meant to Joe."

"More than his own flesh and blood," he said.

"No, but they were important to him."

"Just like you were. How did you worm your way into his affection?"

This was going nowhere good. "Just let me go, Bobby, and sleep it off. Tomorrow you'll see that Joe gave you a future to look forward to."

"I won't let those McCullens cut me out of what I'm owed."

Scarlet's heart pounded. That sounded like a threat. "Don't do anything stupid."

"Why do you keep defending them? They might contest the will so you don't get that money, either."

"I'm not defending anyone," Scarlet said. "I'm trying to honor Joe's wishes."

"Here's what you're going to do," Bobby said in a hoarse tone next to her ear. "You're going to sign your money and land over to me. That's only fair, Scarlet, since I shared my daddy with you. After all, you're not a McCullen and you never will be."

RAY THREW HIS Range Rover into Park in front of Scarlet's office building, then hurried up to the front door. Hugh met him on the outside stoop.

"Deputy Whitefeather said that you called about Scarlet. Did she ever make it?"

"No. And I'm afraid that awful man Lloyd Pullman got her."

"I'll take a look around." Ray eased down the steps and scanned the parking lot, listening for sounds. Scarlet's voice. A cry for help.

Nothing.

The car Scarlet had been driving was parked in the small parking lot beside a sedan and a minivan that probably belonged to her coworker and the client. He didn't spot any other vehicles, which worried him more.

If Pullman was here, had he abducted her and driven off?

A vacant building sat beside the office. He inched to the corner of the building and peeked around, ears straining for any sign of Scarlet or Pullman. One step at a time, he crept down the alley, pausing to listen every few feet.

Suddenly he heard a voice. Low. Angry.

"You're going to do it, Scarlet."

Not Pullman. Bobby.

Remembering he could be violent, Ray slipped his gun from inside his jacket and held it at the ready. One step, two, three, he crept closer until he spotted an overhang from the warehouse and heard Scarlet's voice.

"Bobby, it doesn't have to be like this—"

"Shut up, Scarlet. You're going back to work and call that lawyer and make the arrangements."

Ray eased from the shadows of the awning, his gun raised. Fury heated his blood when he saw the way Bobby had trapped her against the wall. "Let her go, Bobby." He aimed his weapon at the man's head. *"Now."*

Bobby jerked his head up, rage flaming in his eyes, then yanked Scarlet in front of him. Bastard.

"Go ahead, shoot."

Ray's gaze met Scarlet's. Fear clouded her expression, but she lifted her chin in a show of courage.

"This is not what our father wanted," Ray said.

Bobby cursed again. "Our father was a two-timing jerk who led my mother on for years and treated us like a second-tier family."

"I don't know why he did what he did," Ray said. "But Scarlet had nothing to do with Dad's choices."

"Yes, she did," Bobby snapped. "He chose to take care of her like she was his blood, when he left me all the time to go back to you and your brothers."

"That must have sucked," Ray said. "But giving you part of Horseshoe Creek and forcing us to work together must have been his way of finally making things right."

Bobby tightened his grip on Scarlet. "How did he think we could work together when we don't even know each other? When he cheated me out of what was mine?"

"Bobby, just let me go and we'll work all this out," Scarlet said in a pleading tone.

"She's right," Ray said. "We'll sit down and talk."

A siren wailed. Deputy Whitefeather on his way.

Panic lit Bobby's eyes, and he shoved Scarlet to the ground. She hit the cement with a yelp, and Ray ran forward to help her up.

"Scarlet," Ray said.

"I'm fine." She brushed her hair from her face just as the deputy's car screeched to a halt.

"Tell Whitefeather I'm going after Bobby."
Then Ray broke into a sprint.

SCARLET WAS TREMBLING as she walked toward the
front of the building. Hugh rushed outside to greet
her, and Deputy Whitefeather climbed from his
police-issued SUV and strode toward her. "Miss
Lovett?"

"I'm okay," Scarlet said as he met up with her.

"Did Pullman hurt you?" Hugh asked.

She shook her head. "It wasn't Pullman. Bobby
cornered me."

"Bobby?" the deputy asked.

"He's sort of my adopted brother," she said.
"Ray can explain. He went after him."

"Do you need an ambulance?" Deputy Whitefeather asked.

"No." She massaged her wrist where Bobby
had twisted it.

Ray raced around the corner then, his breathing choppy. "Damn. He got away. He was parked
on the other side of the warehouse."

"I'll issue a BOLO on him," Deputy Whitefeather said.

"I'm not sure that's necessary," Scarlet said.
"He just needs time to cool down."

"Scarlet, you can't let him get away with this,"
Ray said.

"I agree," Hugh interjected. "He's no better
than Pullman."

They were right. She should follow through.
But doing so would only fuel his animosity.
    Then he might try to hurt Ray.

Chapter Nineteen

Bobby wouldn't get away with bullying Scarlet. Ray didn't care if they were blood related or not.

A real man didn't exert force on a woman for any reason. Period.

"Issue the APB, pick him up and bring him in," Ray said. "I'll update Maddox."

The deputy gave a clipped nod, then angled his head toward Scarlet. "Let me know if you hear from him or Pullman again."

Scarlet agreed, and the deputy left. Hugh moved closer. "You want me to drive you home, Scarlet? I'll be glad to stay with you."

"No, thanks, Hugh. But I think I'll get some files and work at home this evening."

Ray didn't miss the disappointment in the man's eyes when Scarlet pulled away from him.

Not that it should bother him if Hugh was interested or if she reciprocated his affection. He and

Scarlet were just…what? Friends? Acquaintances? Two people who shared a love for his father?

Scarlet ducked inside the office, and Hugh trailed her as if he needed to be close to her. Ray followed them both, his eyes glued to Scarlet as she quickly gathered her files.

Bobby was still on the loose and Pullman was a wild card. He didn't intend to leave her alone and let either one of them get to her.

SCARLET STRUGGLED TO hold herself together as she gathered her files. Thankfully nothing was pressing at the moment.

Besides, she needed some time to figure out what to do about Bobby. Her experience as a social worker warned her that she needed to press charges, that allowing Bobby to get away with accosting her was abuse.

But he was Joe's son and Barbara would hate her if she pressed charges. They were the only two family members Scarlet had left.

If only Bobby would do as Joe requested and enter into rehab, he might finally let go of his anger and move on with his life. He and the McCullens might even learn to accept each other one day and be the family Joe had wanted.

You made a mess, Joe.

She could almost hear him whispering back

that he knew it. But that he was hoping she could bridge the gap and pull his two families together.

A sarcastic laugh bubbled in her throat. *Too much to ask.*

"Ready?" Ray's deep voice reverberated with concern, causing a pang in her chest. She was more accustomed to rejection than having someone treat her with tenderness.

"Yes, just a minute." She locked her file drawer, then turned to Hugh. "Let me know if anything important comes up."

Hugh nodded, although he looked sullen as if he was pouting over the fact that she'd turned down his offer to stay with her. Knowing he'd had a hard life himself, and that he'd been a good friend, Scarlet leaned over and gave him a quick hug.

Hugh had been rejected so many times in his life that she needed to be gentle. One day he'd find someone special that he belonged with.

She looked up at Ray, and her heart stuttered. Ray was the strong, rugged masculine type that made her hungry for sex. The protective type who made her feel safe.

The intensely caring type that made her dream about love.

But he would be leaving Pistol Whip soon.

Or would he? He'd inherited a third of Horseshoe Creek. Was there a chance that he'd stay and run it with his brothers?

A chance that he might learn to love her?

RAY CLENCHED HIS hands by his side, jealousy rearing its ugly head again. That smile was the only encouragement a man like Hugh needed to think he might win Scarlet's heart.

Ray had no idea why that irked him so much, but it did. Scarlet deserved someone strong and loving, someone who wanted a family, someone who understood her commitment to the kids at The Family Farm and the pain she'd suffered.

Hugh might fit that bill, though.

Still, he wasn't the man for Scarlet because…

Because why? He wanted her for himself?

That thought bounced around in his head as he followed her back to her house. He checked over his shoulder as he drove, well aware that either Pullman or Bobby might show up again.

Not that he didn't have his own enemies. He still had no idea who'd caused his crash and beaten the hell out of him. Or who'd set the fire at the horse barn. Arlis Bennett? Hardwick or Romley?

Bobby?

Bobby hadn't beaten him up, but he could have paid someone to do it. Maybe one of his hoodlum buddies?

He phoned Maddox to fill him in before he arrived at Scarlet's.

"Bobby attacked Scarlet?" Maddox said, his voice irritated.

"Yes. Whitefeather issued an APB for him."

Maddox muttered a sound of frustration. "This is a cluster."

Ray felt sorry for his older brother. At least he'd grown up with no illusions about their father being the perfect hero. Maddox had.

"I'll dig up everything I can on Bobby," Maddox said.

Ray relayed the charges on Bobby's rap sheet. "That's one reason Dad placed those stipulations on his share."

Worse, their father had tied them to Bobby Lowman and Barbara for the rest of their lives.

Scarlet might be the only gem in this tangled mess.

"Brett explained about the barn fire and Romley," Maddox said. "I'm going to question Hardwick at the hospital. Maybe he knows more than he admitted to you."

Ray sighed. "Whitefeather was researching Bennett's financials for a connection between him and Romley but hasn't found one."

"I talked to him," Maddox said. "The DNA on that cigarette butt was inconclusive."

Before they hung up, they agreed to keep each other posted. Scarlet parked, and he rolled in beside her and cut the engine. It took her a minute to gather her briefcase, then she locked the car and walked up the steps to the front door.

She glanced over her shoulder at him as he climbed from his Range Rover, and his heart lurched. She looked so fragile and beautiful, a tempting combination.

He hurried up the steps behind her. She dropped her briefcase on the table by the door, then flipped on a light. The tentative smile she offered him flooded his body with heat.

Her face looked pale though, and she gave a little shiver as if she was remembering her altercation with Bobby.

"I'm going to shower," she said, her voice cracking as she passed the kitchen and living room and crossed the hallway to her bedroom.

A second later, Scarlet's scream sent him running.

SCARLET STARED IN horror at her bed. At the doll…

"What's wrong?" Ray rushed in, weapon drawn, and pulled her behind him. "Is someone here?"

"No…I don't know." Scarlet pointed to the porcelain doll Joe had given her. It was so beautiful and reminded her of the day he'd told her he considered her his daughter.

Now that porcelain face was completely shattered.

An image of that burned photo flashed behind her eyes. Had the same person who'd left it smashed the doll's face?

Ray glanced at the doll, then quickly checked the closet and bathroom to make sure no one was inside. "It's clear," he said as he returned.

"But someone was here," Scarlet said, agitated. "Someone who knew what that doll meant to me." Someone who wanted to hurt her.

She retrieved the envelope with the photo in it and showed it to Ray. His gaze met hers, hot with anger. "Where did you get this?"

"Hugh said he found it at the office. Someone slid it under the door. I meant to give it to the deputy but forgot."

"I'll have Maddox send it and the doll to the lab. Bobby isn't going to get away with terrorizing you like this."

Scarlet wanted to cry out at the injustice of the situation, but she was trembling instead, and tears trickled down her cheeks.

"I never meant to ruin his life," she said, talking out loud. "But he resented me from the beginning."

Ray muttered a curse, his boots clicking on the wood floor as he strode over to her. "You didn't do anything wrong," he said in a gruff voice. "And you certainly didn't ruin his life. He's doing that himself."

Pain wrenched Scarlet's heart. "All I ever

wanted was a family," she said. "To be wanted like the other kids."

But Bobby hadn't wanted her. And neither had Barbara.

And now Bobby was determined to destroy her.

To avoid interfering with fingerprints, Ray used the afghan to move the doll to the dresser. Then he gently laid his gun on the end table.

"I can't believe he hates me so much," she said.

Ray stroked her back in small circles. "I'm sorry for how you grew up, Scarlet, but my father obviously loved you or he wouldn't have given you that doll. And he wouldn't have left you that cabin and a piece of his land. That meant more to him than the money because it was part of the McCullen legacy."

She'd thought the same thing. But…today had just been too much. Bobby wouldn't stop until he ran her out of town.

"I understand that your father made mistakes and you're all disappointed with him," Scarlet said, sensitive to their side. "But he was a good man deep down, Ray. No matter what happens, I'm glad he was in my life."

Emotions darkened Ray's expression, and he pulled her up against him. "Nothing is going to happen to you, Scarlet." He tilted his head to the side, his eyes heated, stormy.

And so sexy that Scarlet lost herself in the brown depths.

"I promise I'll protect you," he murmured. "Bobby won't hurt you as long as I'm around."

Her heart fluttered, the fear that had gripped her in its clutches slowly dissipating as his warm, strong arms surrounded her. Her body tingled with desire as he cradled her next to his chest.

Then he fused his mouth with hers. He tasted like honey and sex and the forbidden, everything she'd ever wanted in a man but had tried to resist.

She couldn't resist any longer.

Scarlet lifted one hand and slipped his Stetson off and dropped it into the chair by the bed, then tunneled her fingers through his thick dark hair. He deepened the kiss, probing her lips apart with his tongue, and she willingly gave in to him, tearing at his shirt to get closer to his hard, male body and the strength beneath.

RAY FORGOT ALL the reasons he shouldn't kiss Scarlet as her tongue danced with his. His body was on fire from wanting her. That hungry craving inside him couldn't be satisfied until he tasted and touched every inch of her.

She tore at his shirt, and he tugged at hers, his pulse pounding at the sight of the lacy bra barely covering her generous breasts. Her breath rushed out in a tortured sigh as if she needed him as much as he needed her, and he lowered her to the bed, crawled on top of her and kissed her again, telling her with his mouth that he intended to love her.

Chapter Twenty

Scarlet's body tingled with every touch of Ray's hands. He deepened the kiss, his body brushing hers in a sensual invitation.

She answered by rubbing her foot up and down his calf and meeting his tongue thrust with her own.

Except she wanted more. Wanted his clothes off so she could feel her foot against his bare leg. Her breasts against the hard planes of his chest. His skin against her own.

He trailed kisses along her neck and throat, causing her to shiver with longing, and she ran her fingers over his bare shoulders, savoring the way his muscles bunched and flexed against her hands.

Heat spiraled through her as he teased the sensitive area behind her ear, and his hands slid down to rub her breasts through her lacy bra. Her nipples stiffened, aching and begging for more, and he stripped her bra and closed his lips over one turgid tip.

She sighed in pleasure and ran her fingers over his bare skin urging him closer. He loved one breast then the other, suckling her until she felt the tugging sensations of an orgasm deep in her womb.

Desperate for more, she pulled at his jeans and, seconds later, they both stripped and lay naked in each other's arms. She had never seen such a handsome, virile man. His muscular physique robbed her breath and made her feel things she'd never felt before—the kind of aching hunger that needed sating and could only be satisfied by him.

Her breasts brushed his chest, titillating her even more, and he skimmed his fingers down her back to her waist, then lower to her hips. She undulated, desperate to be more intimate, and he kissed her again, deeply and more passionately than she'd ever been kissed.

He stroked her backside, then trailed more hot, hungry kisses down her throat and torso, pausing to love each inch of her as he stirred her desires. Another kiss in her navel, then his lips skated downward until she felt him drop tender love licks along her inner thighs.

She groaned his name and parted her legs, her body humming to life as he teased her sweet spot with his fingers and then his mouth.

Hot pleasure washed over her, and she quivered as he loved her, a dozen mindless sensations shooting through her as her passion exploded into sweet release.

THE SOUND OF Scarlet's erotic whisper of pleasure sparked Ray's hunger. She tasted like sweetness and woman, a heady taste that whetted his appetite for more.

His sex hardened, throbbing for release, and he rose above her and cupped her face in one hand while he braced his weight on the other. Her eyes were glazed with passion, her lips plump and swollen from his kisses, a sight that he imprinted in his brain forever.

An urgency throbbed within him as she kissed him again and slipped one hand down to cup his erection. He couldn't resist. He thrust himself at her center, and she guided him toward her. But when the tip of his hard body touched her intimately, he suddenly remembered protection.

"Condom." She nodded and he lifted away from her and grabbed a foil packet from his jeans. He tore it open with his teeth, then she took it from him and helped him roll it on.

Her fingers against his bare skin was so titillating he thought he might explode in her hands. But he sucked in a breath, wanting to be inside her when he climaxed.

She stroked his back, then trailed her hands down his hips and over his butt and urged him between her thighs. He teased her center with his thick length, stroking her until she whispered for him to enter her.

Need and passion mingled with emotions that he'd never felt before. He was touched and honored to be in Scarlet's bed.

But he didn't have time to contemplate those feelings as she raked her nails over his back and guided him inside her. He filled her, then paused, allowing her a moment to adjust to his size. She was so tight that he didn't want to hurt her.

She moaned his name, and he fused his mouth with hers and kissed her again, this time thrusting his sex deeper, then withdrawing. Over and over he teased her until she clutched his hips.

"I need you," she whispered against his neck.

"I need you, too," he said, surprising himself when he realized that he meant it on more than one level.

She undulated her hips against him and wrapped her legs around him, and once again he forgot to think as he lost himself in the rhythm.

His lungs strained for air as he intensified his movements, driving deeper and deeper inside her until she cried out his name and another orgasm claimed her. Her body tightened around his, stroking his length until his own release teetered on the surface. Another kiss, then another moan and her pleasure triggered his own, and he spilled his seed inside her.

He pumped and thrust harder and faster, his heart racing as the two of them clung to each other.

SCARLET CLUNG TO Ray as the aftermath of their lovemaking lingered. She felt languid and happy and hungry, as if she already wanted more.

The thought terrified her. She hadn't had many relationships at all with men, had kept them at bay, unable to trust in their motives or affections. But with Ray, rational thought went by the wayside.

His heavy breathing bathed her neck as he moaned against her. She smiled and kissed his neck, sensations still rippling through her. He lifted himself from her and disappeared into the bathroom, and she suddenly felt bereft.

Was he going to leave now?

But he crawled back in bed with her and pulled her into his arms. She snuggled up next to him, easing her head into the crook of his shoulder as if that was where she belonged.

Ray twirled a strand of her hair between his fingers and toyed with it, and she rubbed his chest with her fingers, tangling them in the fine dark mat of hair on his chest. The moment was sweet and tender and made her feel closer to him than she'd ever felt with anyone.

They lay there holding and touching and caressing each other for what seemed like forever. At least she *wanted* it to last forever.

The wind whistled outside, banging a tree branch against the window, but instead of startling her, she closed her eyes, cocooned in the warmth of Ray's arms. Nothing could hurt her or frighten her as long as they were entwined.

But sometime later, Ray's phone buzzed from his jeans' pocket. She bit her lip, hoping he wouldn't answer it and break the intimate spell around them. It buzzed again though, and Ray hissed.

"I guess I'd better get that. It might be about Bobby or Pullman."

Hearing both men's names sent a shiver up her spine. Ray must have felt it because he hugged her again, then planted a kiss on her lips. "Don't move."

His words warmed her with the promise that he planned to return to her bed. He stood, and she had no shame about looking at his handsome muscular physique. He glanced down and noticed her attention to his sex, which was jutting out, ready and engorged, and he grinned.

"I said, don't move."

She laughed softly and hugged the pillow to her as he snatched his phone.

Just as he answered it, the doorbell dinged. Ray frowned at her in question, and she shrugged, then slipped from bed, grabbed her robe and tugged it on.

She pushed her tangled hair from her face,

tightening the belt of her robe as she walked into the living room. She peeked through the front sheers and saw Hugh's car.

Relieved it wasn't Bobby or Pullman, but irritated at the interruption, she opened the door. "Hugh, what are you doing here?"

Hugh elbowed his way inside. "I knew you were upset about Bobby's attack and wanted to check on you."

Hadn't he seen Ray's car in the drive?

"I told you I'm fine."

Hugh's jaw twitched. He looked more agitated than usual. "Did something happen after I left, Hugh?"

"No, I just thought you might need me. Was your house okay when you got home?"

Scarlet's pulse jumped as she remembered the broken doll. "Why would you ask that?"

He shrugged, his thin lips forming a pout. "I just wondered. Didn't you get a locksmith to change your locks?"

"How did you know that?"

Hugh fidgeted. "You told me, don't you remember?"

Scarlet searched her memory. The past few days had been hectic and unsettling as she'd dealt with Ray, the McCullens, Pullman, Bobby and Barbara.

"I did have new locks," Scarlet said. "But as you

see, I'm fine." In fact, she wanted him to leave so she could go back to Ray.

Speaking of Ray, he strode in, his jeans slung low on his hips as he buttoned his shirt.

Hugh made a disgusted sound in his throat. "So, this is how it is?"

Scarlet tensed at the edge to his tone.

Ray dragged on his jacket, then jammed his gun inside the interior pocket. "Hugh?"

"I was worried about Scarlet," Hugh said.

Ray glanced at Scarlet. "I have to go. Deputy Whitefeather has a lead on Bobby. Maddox is going to meet us at the location."

"I'll go with you," Scarlet said.

"No, it might be dangerous." Ray gestured toward Hugh.

"I'll stay with her while you're gone," Hugh offered eagerly.

Scarlet's temper reared its head. "I don't need a babysitter."

"No, you need a bodyguard," Ray said.

Scarlet caught Ray's arm. "Please, Ray, I'll go with you."

Ray's gaze met hers, the memory of their lovemaking still vivid in her mind. She wanted to go back to bed with him, not entertain Hugh.

Ray traced his finger down her cheek in a tender gesture. "I'll be back when we have Bobby in custody. Meanwhile lock the door."

Scarlet bit her tongue to keep from begging him to stay as he left her alone with her coworker.

RAY MADE IT to The Silver Bullet before Deputy Whitefeather. In fact, Whitefeather phoned and said the sheriff in Laramie had Pullman in custody. Apparently he'd caught Pullman attempting to steal a car. The man had been so loaded he'd admitted that he was going to hijack the vehicle, then steal his daughter and leave town.

Scarlet would be relieved to know he was in jail. This time he faced felony charges and wouldn't be released in a day or two, either.

The parking lot of the Silver Bullet was nearly full, country music blaring from the speakers as he stepped from his vehicle. He scouted out the exterior but didn't see Lowman, so he checked the alley to make sure he wasn't hiding out.

Hopefully Bobby had no idea the bartender had phoned Whitefeather. But Whitefeather had been smart enough to figure that if Bobby liked booze, he might show up at the closest bar in town tonight to drown his sorrows, so he'd alerted his friend.

Ray's senses were honed as he entered the bar, scanning the crowd for Bobby. Johnny Cash's voice boomed over the speaker, a line dance was in motion on the dance floor and the pool tables and dartboard corner were packed.

Ray eased his way through the crowd, avoiding eye contact with a redhead who gave him a flirtatious smile. He inched up to the bar and motioned to the bartender.

"You called the deputy about Bobby Lowman?"

The young man nodded and gestured to the back corner where a young man in a black leather jacket stood near the rear exit. Lowman slipped some cash from his wallet, and shoved it into the man's hands.

Then Lowman reached out his hand and the man laid a .38 special in his palm. Ray tensed, dropping back behind a group of cowboys so Bobby wouldn't see him.

Ray kept his cool and waited, then watched Lowman slip out the back exit. Determined not to let Bobby escape, especially now that he was armed, Ray wove through the crowd and eased out the back.

Gravel crunched as his boots hit the parking lot, the wind carrying the scent of garbage, stale booze and cigarette smoke. Three cowboys were huddled around a truck bed smoking, a woman and man were necking under the awning of the neighboring building and a truck engine fired up.

Expecting it to be Bobby, Ray left his cover and dashed to the right to see the license, but a bullet zinged by his head.

Ray ducked behind the corner and pivoted to see the shooter's location just as another bullet pierced his hat.

Chapter Twenty-One

Scarlet folded her arms, anxious to get rid of Hugh. "I thought you were working this afternoon, Hugh. I need you to make sure everything at the office is going smoothly."

"Don't worry, everything is in good shape at work. But you seemed so upset earlier, I had to see you." Hugh reached out and rubbed her arm.

Uncomfortable with the way he was looking at her, she stepped into the kitchen. "How about some coffee or tea?"

"Coffee would be great."

She nodded, pulled a filter from the cabinet, measured the coffee and poured the water in. Seconds later, the deep, rich scent of hickory filled the air, soothing her nerves. Ray was going to find Bobby and things would be all right.

"I had a meeting with a couple who are interested in adopting Rachelle."

Hope budded in Scarlet's chest. Rachelle reminded her of herself at that age. Small, slightly sickly, shy. Lonely. She was ten and had asthma but she was a sweet little girl who needed a loving home. "That's great. What did you think of the couple?"

"They're nice, stable and say they want an older child. The father is a pharmacist, the wife is a tutor at a child learning center."

"That sounds promising." Scarlet poured them both coffee and handed Hugh a mug.

"What's going on with you and that McCullen man?" Hugh asked.

Scarlet blew on her coffee. "It's complicated, Hugh."

"He's Joe's son. We both know Joe cheated on his wife. You think his son will be any better?"

Scarlet inhaled sharply. She hadn't realized Hugh harbored animosity toward Joe. "Where is this coming from, Hugh? Joe helped you at the orphanage just like he did me."

"He took you away from me," Hugh said in a low voice.

Scarlet stared at him in shock. "That's not true, Hugh. He gave me a home, that's all."

"But you left The Family Farm and I was alone."

She wanted to argue that there had been ten other kids in the home at the time. But she knew exactly what he meant. Even in a crowded room, you could feel very much alone.

"I'm sorry, Hugh, I never realized you felt that way."

Pain flashed in his eyes. "I thought we were a team," he said. "That we were inseparable."

"Hugh, we were kids. The past ten years we've both grown up. We have a good partnership at the social services agency."

Hugh moved toward her and set his coffee on the counter. "But we can be so much more, Scarlet."

Scarlet placed her coffee beside his. She had to be gentle. "Hugh, I like you as a friend and co-worker, but that's all there can be between us."

A frown pulled at Hugh's thin face. "Because you're in love with Ray McCullen?"

Yes. But Scarlet had no idea where things stood with Ray, or where they were going.

"This is not about Ray," Scarlet said.

"You need me," Hugh said. "You and I are alike."

"Hugh—"

"Please, Scarlet. I can keep you safe from whoever sent that picture and from the person who smashed your doll."

Scarlet went very still. "How did you know about the doll?"

Hugh's eyes widened. "You told me."

"No, I didn't," Scarlet said. "I just found it when I got home earlier."

Hugh's eye twitched. "Well…you did mention it. You must have forgotten."

"No, Hugh, I didn't." The hair on the back of her neck prickled. Hugh had given her that envelope with the burned picture inside.

And the doll—he knew Joe had given it to her. Was Hugh trying to frighten her into his arms?

RAY DODGED ANOTHER BULLET, crouching low and straining to catch a glimpse of Bobby. "Give it up, man," Ray shouted.

Footsteps pounded and he glanced around the corner and saw Bobby heading toward a pickup. More footsteps sounded, and Maddox barreled into the alley, pausing, his weapon drawn.

Ray pointed to the rear parking lot. "He has a truck in the back."

"Stay behind me." Maddox held his gun at the ready and led the way down the alley. Another bullet pinged off the brick wall as they crept to the end. Bobby made a run for his truck, putting him out in the open.

Maddox stepped from the corner of the building and aimed his gun. "Stop, Lowman, or I'll shoot."

Bobby dove for the truck though, forcing Maddox to act. He fired a shot, the bullet pinging the ground at Bobby's feet. That made the man freeze and throw up his hands in surrender.

"Don't move," Maddox ordered as he inched forward. Ray provided backup, his own gun aimed at Bobby.

"You're really going to take your own brother to jail?" Bobby's angry words were slurred as he turned to face them.

"You shot at us," Ray said.

Maddox kept his gun aimed at Bobby's chest to make sure the man didn't try to shoot again or run.

Rage oozed from Bobby's pores, mingling with the stench of alcohol.

Eyes focused on Bobby, Maddox lifted Bobby's .38 from his hand and tucked it in the waistband of his jeans.

"I wasn't trying to kill nobody," Bobby muttered. "I just wanted you to leave me alone."

"Just like you didn't try to hurt Scarlet," Ray said, not bothering to hide his disdain.

Maddox unhooked the handcuffs from his belt, jerked Bobby's hands behind him, spun him around and snapped the handcuffs around his wrists. "A few nights in jail might be good for you."

"I don't belong in jail," Bobby wailed. "I should have been a McCullen."

"You jerk," Maddox growled. "Our father gave you a chance when he willed that land to you. But you aren't going to get it this way."

Bobby jerked against the cuffs. "That bitch

Scarlet doesn't have to do anything, he just gave it to her and she's not even family."

Ray barely contained his animosity toward Bobby as he jammed his gun in his jacket. "Scarlet has nothing to do with this. This is about you. If you want to be part of the McCullens, then start acting like one."

"But—"

"He's right," Maddox said as he gave Bobby a shove. "McCullen men don't go around beating up and harassing women. And they sure as hell don't go on drunk tears and shoot at the law. Hell, Bobby, you could have killed Ray or some innocent bystander."

Bobby protested, but Maddox pushed him through the alley between the buildings. When they reached the front parking lot, a few patrons were leaving The Silver Bullet and paused to watch, looking guarded as Maddox opened the back door to his police SUV and pushed Bobby inside.

Ray's phone buzzed and he checked it, worried about Scarlet. But Brett's number appeared. He punched Connect.

"Yeah?"

"Ray, there's another fire!"

Ray clenched the phone in a white-knuckled grip. "Where?"

"The house. I called the fire department."

"Maddox is here with me. We'll be right there."

Maddox froze, brows furrowed. "What the hell's wrong?"

"The house is on fire." Ray snatched his keys from his pocket and jogged toward his Range Rover.

Maddox's eyes glittered with panic. "God, Rose is home." He wrenched open his car door. "Follow me." Maddox jumped in the vehicle, flipped on the siren and sped from the parking lot.

Ray followed, praying no one was hurt.

SCARLET DIDN'T LIKE the dark road her thoughts had taken. She and Hugh had known each other for years. They'd been friends. Coworkers.

He also suffered from depression and took medication for bipolar disorder to control his erratic mood swings.

How could she have missed the signs that he was more troubled lately? That he might have developed an unhealthy attachment to her?

She massaged her temple, feigning a headache. "Hugh, I appreciate you coming, but I'm really tired and need a nap."

"Let me hold you while you rest." Hugh reached for her hand. Her skin crawled, but she forced herself not to react.

"That's sweet, Hugh, but I need to be alone." She took his hand and led him toward the door. "Keep me updated on that couple who want to adopt Rachelle."

He stood at the door, his hand gripping hers a little too tightly. "Please let me stay, Scarlet. We've been good friends forever. We can be more."

"I'm sorry, Hugh," Scarlet said. "There's too much going on in my life for me to have a relationship with anyone."

His mouth settled into a thin line. "What about Ray McCullen?"

She swallowed hard. "Ray and I met to discuss his father's will. Joe left money for The Family Farm, and I wanted to make sure the McCullens didn't contest it."

"Really? Is that all there is to it?" he asked, his voice laced with suspicion. "Because it looked like more."

She wanted more. But what did Ray want?

"Yes," she said, careful not to antagonize Hugh. "Now, please, let me lie down. I'll call you later."

He reluctantly stepped outside, and she peered through the window to make sure that he drove away.

Then she reached for the phone to call Ray. Hugh's fingerprints would definitely be on the envelope he'd given her with that burned photo inside. But what about the doll?

If his fingerprints were on it, she'd know that he was the one who'd smashed it.

RAY'S PHONE BUZZED just as he veered onto the drive leading to the ranch house. Fear seized him at the sight of the smoke curling upward in the distance.

Maddox bounced over the dirt road, gravel flying, his siren roaring.

The phone buzzed again and he snatched it up. When he saw Scarlet's name, panic bubbled inside, and he connected the call. "Scarlet?"

"Yes, did you get Bobby?"

"Yeah, he's in handcuffs in Maddox's car, but there's a fire at the ranch. We're on our way there now."

"Oh, my God," Scarlet gasped.

Ray spun down the drive, the smoke thickening as he drew closer. Flames shot into the sky, lighting it with orange and red. He had to go. "Are you okay?"

"Yes. How did the fire start?"

"I don't know. I'll call you back when I find out more." Satisfied she was safe with Pullman and Bobby in custody, he hung up, then swung to a stop behind Maddox in the drive.

"Rose!" Maddox threw the car door open and jumped out, sprinting toward the house. Ray followed suit, grief pummeling him at the sight of their homestead in flames. The left side where the master bedroom was located was engulfed, and the flames were spreading to the living area.

The firefighters were already working to roll out the hoses and douse the flames.

"Rose!" Maddox shouted over the roar.

Ray scanned the front yard and spotted Brett talking to one of the firefighters.

"Rose!" Maddox yelled again.

Rose emerged from the side of an ambulance, a blanket wrapped around her, and ran toward Maddox. He hauled her into his arms, his shoulders shaking with emotions as they hugged.

Relief flooded Ray when he saw Mama Mary standing by the ambulance, and he jogged over to her.

She threw her arms around him, her big body trembling. "Lordy, Mr. Ray, I can't believe this. We can't lose your daddy's house!"

"Don't worry about the house, Mama Mary." Ray tightened his grip on her. He couldn't have stood to lose her. "I'm just glad you're okay."

Tears streamed down her face, and she hugged him and kissed his cheek. Finally she pulled back, drying her eyes and swiping her hair into its bun.

Ray cleared his throat, his own eyes stinging. "What happened? How did the fire start?"

"I don't know," Mama Mary said. "Miss Rose was at work. She said she and Mr. Maddox were going out for dinner tonight, so I went to my church supper. When I got here, Miss Rose was pulling up. Smoke was pouring from the house so we ran inside to see if it was the stove, but the smoke was so thick we couldn't see anything, and flames were in the bedroom." She heaved for a breath. "Rose called 911, then she grabbed the fire extinguisher, and I tried beating it out with a blanket, but it was spreading too fast."

Ray took a deep breath and squeezed her arm. "I'm just glad you weren't hurt."

Maddox and Rose joined them, Maddox's face etched with love for his new wife.

"I'm so sorry, Ray," Rose said. "Mama Mary and I tried to put it out."

"Don't worry about it," Ray said. "We're just grateful the two of you are safe."

"You don't know what started the fire?" Ray asked.

Rose shook her head. "No, but I...thought I smelled gas."

"Like the stove was left on?" Maddox asked.

"I didn't leave the stove on," Mama Mary's voice quivered. "At least I don't think I did."

"No, not the stove," Rose said. "Like gasoline."

Ray and Maddox exchanged looks. "The same person who set the barn fire probably started this one."

Maddox hauled Rose close for a kiss. "Let me look around. See if we find anything suspicious."

He glanced at Bobby. Bobby was staring at the fire as if he was mesmerized.

But Bobby had been at the bar when the fire started. If he hadn't set it, who had?

SCARLET PUNCHED THE accelerator, anxious to reach Horseshoe Creek. Had Bobby set fire to the ranch house to hurt Ray and his brothers?

The wind picked up outside, shaking tree limbs and tossing tumbleweed across the road as she veered down the drive. She thought she spotted a vehicle behind some bushes, but sped on, worried for the McCullens.

Smoke billowed in the darkening sky, flames lighting the darkness as she approached. Ray's Range Rover and Maddox's police car were parked in the drive, the fire engine close to the house.

Bobby was inside the back of the police SUV, staring at the blaze, a sinister smile on his face.

Scarlet shivered, threw the car into Park and reached for the door.

Another car barreled down the drive and screeched to a stop behind her. She glanced in her rearview mirror and saw Barbara slide from her BMW and walk toward Maddox's vehicle.

Scarlet stepped from her car and faced Barbara. "What are you doing here?"

"I came to talk to the McCullens about how they're treating my son."

"Barbara, for God's sake, now isn't the time. Their house is on fire." She grabbed Barbara's arm, but the woman shoved her away.

"Stay out of this, Scarlet." Barbara stopped beside her son, then jerked the door open.

Maddox and Ray strode toward her.

"What the hell are you doing?" Maddox shouted.

"Scarlet?" Ray said.

Before she could respond, Barbara pulled a gun from her purse and aimed it at her.

Barbara turned a sinister look at Ray and Maddox. "Let my son go or she's dead."

Chapter Twenty-Two

Ray's gut pinched at the sight of Barbara aiming that gun at Scarlet.

"What are you doing, Barbara?" Scarlet said.

"My son was neglected, and now you McCullens are ganging up on him," Barbara shouted over the roar of the blaze.

Ray held up a hand to calm Barbara. "He attacked Scarlet, Barbara. He also opened fire at me. He's a grown man. He has to answer for that."

She kept the gun trained on them, yanked open the back door and motioned for Bobby to get out. He slid from the vehicle, a smile on his face. "Hey, Mom."

Barbara frowned. "I'll deal with you later, son."

She swung the gun toward Maddox. "Give me the handcuff keys."

"What are you going to do, Barbara? Run?" Maddox asked. "Then you and Bobby will never get what Dad left you."

Hatred glistened in Barbara's eyes. "My son should have had equal shares with you. And your father should have married me."

"Barbara, Joe only wanted Bobby to get help," Scarlet said.

Ray's lungs squeezed for air as she turned the gun on Scarlet again. "And you...you played on Joe's sympathy and robbed my son of time with his father." She angled her head toward him and Maddox. "You are such fools, just like Joe. You fell for Scarlet's sweet little act. But she's the one who got my Bobby into trouble when they were young."

Scarlet gasped. "Barbara, that's not true."

"Of course it is. You talked Bobby into breaking into that rich lady's house and stealing her jewelry." She addressed Maddox. "You're the sheriff. I'm sure you investigated her, didn't you? That's what you do. Find out everyone's background so you can protect the McCullens."

Ray's head jerked toward Maddox, and guilt flashed in his oldest brother's eyes. "Maddox?"

"She was arrested when she was a juvenile."

Scarlet paled and bit down on her lip. "That was a mistake. Bobby lied and implicated me in a break-in, but I was cleared."

Ray didn't know what to believe. He couldn't imagine the sweet, giving woman he knew doing anything illegal, although she had had a troubled childhood.

Barbara waved the gun toward Maddox. "Now, you're going to do the right thing. You're going to unlock those handcuffs and let us drive away. Then you're going to drop the charges against Bobby and give us what's owed us with no strings attached."

Maddox inched forward. "You're not helping your son by doing this, Barbara. He'll just keep on drinking and hurting other people. Dad didn't want that."

Barbara released a sardonic laugh. "Funny how he couldn't get past Bobby drinking, but he sure as hell covered up for your mother."

Ray's heart hammered and Maddox went still. Brett had joined them, his look confused. "What does that mean?" Ray asked.

"Your daddy lied to you about me. I was the good one. Your mama was the one who couldn't hold her liquor."

"Shut up, Barbara." Mama Mary eased up beside Maddox and folded her arms beneath her ample bosom, facing Barbara like a mama bear protecting her cubs. "Just because he wouldn't marry you doesn't mean you need to hurt these boys."

"They should know the truth," Barbara said. "Maybe they wouldn't be so damn judgmental then."

"What's she talking about, Mama Mary?" Maddox asked.

"Your perfect mother," Barbara said. "She didn't die because a drunk driver hit her. She was the drunk driver. She rammed her own car into a tree and killed herself."

Shock slammed into Ray. Judging from Maddox's curse and Brett's sharp hiss, they were equally stunned.

Behind them, the firefighters were still working to save the McCullen home.

"We're going to walk away and you're going to drop those charges." Barbara snatched the handcuff key from Maddox, then tossed it to Bobby. He quickly unlocked the cuffs, then flung them to the ground.

Barbara backed toward her car, motioning for Bobby to get in. Bobby had to pass Scarlet to reach the passenger side. He paused to tweak her hair and give her a gloating look. "Finally you'll get what you deserve. Nothing."

Maddox seemed to have recovered from the shock of Barbara's statement more quickly than Ray. "Did you set this fire, Barbara?"

"Setting fires is not my style, so don't try to pin that on me or my son." She jumped in the car, keeping the gun aimed at them until she revved up the engine. Then she slammed the door and sped away.

Ray took one look at Maddox who already had his keys out. "Stay here and take care of the women," Maddox told Brett. "I'm going after them. They're not going to get away."

Scarlet reached for Ray's arm. "Ray—"

"I'm going with him," Ray said, his emotions all over the place.

Was Scarlet the sweet, innocent woman he'd thought, or had she deceived his father and now him to get her share of the ranch?

SCARLET'S CHEST ACHED as Ray and Maddox followed Barbara and Bobby.

She'd seen the doubt in Ray's eyes. He believed what Barbara said about her leading Bobby into trouble.

Disappointment mixed with anger. All her life she'd fought to be somebody, to fit into a family, to overcome being tossed aside as a child. But Joe had been the only one who'd seen the good in her and loved her.

She'd hoped with Ray...

Brett was watching her as Rose and Mama Mary approached. Needing to leave before she burst into tears, she climbed in her car, but her hands were shaking so badly she dropped the keys on the floor.

The scent of smoke and burned ashes and...betrayal made her head swim. She'd known Barbara resented her and that Bobby was jealous of the attention Joe had given her, but she'd never thought Barbara would lie to punish her. But she had.

Ray's reaction cut to the bone, too.

The flames were dying under the deluge of water the firefighters were dumping on it, but the house was a wreck and would need major renovations.

She found her keys, jammed them in the ignition and started the engine.

Her gaze met Brett's through the front window of her car as she backed up, and everything became clear to her.

She didn't belong here.

She never would.

MADDOX PHONED DEPUTY Whitefeather for backup as he started the SUV, and gave him the license plate for Barbara's car.

"Do you think she was telling the truth about Mom?" Ray asked Maddox as he barreled down the drive to chase Barbara.

A muscle jumped in Maddox's jaw. "I don't know."

"Did Dad ever mention Mom drinking?"

Maddox shook his head, although his silence troubled Ray. He strained to remember his mother as a child, but all he recalled was how beautiful she was. That she made sugar cookies with him and sang to him at night.

"Maddox?"

Maddox released a weary sigh and accelerated, gaining speed on Barbara. "He never talked about it, but now that I think about it, I saw him helping her to bed a few times. I…didn't realize what was happening. But the next day I found an empty vodka bottle by the sofa. Dad saw me with it, and later I heard him and Mom arguing."

So it could be true. Ray felt as if he'd been sucker punched. "Maybe she was drinking because she knew Dad was cheating."

"Maybe," Maddox muttered although he didn't sound convinced. "I don't think we can believe anything Barbara says, though."

Maddox maneuvered a curve, then they spotted Barbara veer down a side road. The SUV bounced over ruts as Maddox flew up on her tail.

"About Scarlet?" Maddox said.

Ray's insides churned. "Yeah, you said she had a record."

"I'm sorry. You like her, don't you?"

He wasn't sure like was the word. He wanted her. He had come to admire her.

He might even…love her.

But had their relationship been based on lies?

"I've got a call in to Judge Winters," Maddox said. "He'll tell me what really went on."

Ray gave a clipped nod, too torn to respond.

Seconds later, they closed in on Barbara. She raced down the road, then disappeared around a curve. Maddox spun around the curve, her lights fading as she increased speed.

Tires squealed as Maddox accelerated, taking

the curve on two wheels. Ahead, he spotted the lights of Barbara's car, then Maddox closed in. Seconds later, she lost control and slammed into a tree.

Maddox jolted to a stop a foot behind her and jumped out, weapon drawn. "Stay in the car," he ordered Ray.

"Hell, no, brother." Ray pulled his own gun from inside his jacket. "I've got your back."

Bobby eased from the car, staggering slightly, and Barbara crawled out, then spun around, weapon aimed. But Maddox was too fast. He jumped her, and they fought for the gun.

Bobby started toward Maddox to help his mother, but Ray tackled him, then shoved his gun in the bastard's face.

"It's over, Bobby. Time to face the music."

Bobby's sinister eyes pierced him. "You'd better not hurt my mother."

A gunshot sounded, and they both froze and glanced sideways.

"Mom!" Bobby shouted.

Ray saw the gun hit the ground, then Maddox pinned Barbara against the side of the car.

"Give it up, Barbara," Maddox growled. "I don't want to hurt you or Bobby, but I'm not going to let you escape, either."

"You owe me, Maddox," Barbara cried. "And Joe owes our son."

"He'll get what he deserves." Maddox tossed

a pair of cuffs toward Ray, and he rolled Bobby over and snapped them on while Maddox cuffed Barbara.

"This isn't fair," Barbara whined. "I deserved his love. She was a drunk."

Maddox said nothing. He shoved her in the back of his squad car, and Ray did the same with Bobby, although Bobby was cursing a blue streak. When they slammed the door, Ray wiped sweat from his forehead.

But Barbara's accusation against their mother taunted him. Mama Mary had commented that their parents had problems. If what Barbara said was true, their father could have turned to Barbara because of their mother's drinking, not the other way around.

If so, he'd been too hard on their father. But their dad should have explained the situation to them when they got older. They would have understood.

Or would they? Ray had already built up such a wall and harbored so much anger that he hadn't given his father a chance.

SCARLET LET HERSELF into her house, chastising herself for getting involved with Ray. She shouldn't have slept with him.

And she certainly shouldn't have fallen in love with him.

Love? Do I love Ray?

Yes. How could she not? He was all the things she'd ever wanted in a man. Strong, handsome, noble...

But he didn't trust her. That doubt in his eyes tore her insides out.

And Ray's brothers...they would never accept her.

So how could she possibly make a home on the piece of land Joe had left her? She would always remind Ray and his brothers of their father's indiscretion. And of his lies.

Why had she ever imagined that she'd fit into their lives?

Or that Ray could love her?

Tears blurred her eyes, but she swiped at them and she made a decision. She took out a pen and pad and began to write.

Dear Ray,
I'm sorry for the trouble my presence in your father's life caused you and your brothers. And I'm sorry that Joe never told you about me or Bobby and Barbara.

I loved your father and I appreciate all that he did for me, more than you'll ever know. But I realize now that I can't make a home on the land that he gave me.

You may not approve, but I do plan to keep the money he designated for The Family Farm.

You and your brothers can reclaim the land
Joe left me as part of Horseshoe Creek. It belongs to your family, not to me.

She started to write Love, Scarlet, but thought
better of it and simply signed her name.

A noise echoed from the back, and Scarlet
froze. She strained to hear, then recognized the
sound. The wind beating a branch against the
glass pane.

Relieved, she stood and walked to the bedroom.
Tomorrow she'd search for a place to move, some-
place that wasn't so close to Pistol Whip and Ray.

Another noise startled her. *The branch again?*
Irritated at herself for being so jumpy, she decided to check it out. But just as she entered her
bedroom and reached out to flip on the light, a
shadow moved in her bathroom.

Scarlet turned to run, but footsteps pounded,
then a man grabbed her from behind.

Chapter Twenty-Three

Deputy Whitefeather met Ray and Maddox at the sheriff's office. Barbara and Bobby continued to deny that they'd set fire to the McCullen house. Both had also denied sending Scarlet the burned photo and smashing her doll.

Then Barbara had evoked her rights to an attorney for her and her son.

"Let's let them sit in jail overnight," Maddox said. "Maybe when Barbara realizes how much trouble she and Bobby are in, she'll confess."

Ray knew he should relax about Scarlet. Barbara, Bobby and Pullman were all in custody.

But a sick feeling knotted his stomach.

He had hurt Scarlet.

"Brett texted that the fire is out," Maddox said. "The arson investigator is there. I want to talk to him."

Deputy Whitefeather nodded. "Go ahead. I'll stay here and hold down the fort."

Ray wanted to get Bobby alone and pound a confession out of him, but Maddox insisted on sticking to the law.

The urge to see Scarlet nagged at Ray.

But he owed his brothers his support. He also wanted to find out who set fire to the house as much as Maddox. Rose or Mama Mary could have been inside and died. And what if Brett's son had been injured?

Ray followed Maddox out the door before he went back in and beat Bobby to a bloody pulp.

Maddox was quiet as they drove to the ranch. "If Bobby and Barbara didn't set fire to the barn and house, who did?"

"Romley is still missing," Ray reminded him.

"True. Hardwick insisted that he was only supposed to report our progress to Bennett, that he wasn't the arsonist. I'm going to find that son of a bitch Romley and get to the truth."

Ray nodded, although his mind wandered back to Scarlet. She'd rushed to the house when she thought they were in trouble, not because she wanted anything from them.

Because she cared.

But when Maddox mentioned her past, a sliver of doubt had crept in.

Not because of Scarlet, but because he had trouble trusting. Seeing his father with another woman had tainted his idea of relationships.

Dammit, he could trust Scarlet. She was the sweetest, most selfless person he'd ever known.

Brett, his family and Rose met them at Maddox's vehicle when they arrived. Rose threw her arms around his brother, obviously grateful to see he'd returned safely.

Maddox pulled away and kissed her. "I'm going to talk to the arson investigator."

Seeing both his brothers happy with their own families triggered a deep-seated loneliness in him.

Making a snap decision, he told Maddox he was going to check on Scarlet. Maddox's dark gaze met his. Brett raised his brows in question.

"You don't want to hear back from that judge first?" Maddox asked.

"I don't need to. I know Scarlet. She deserves everything Dad left her. If you guys don't agree, then I'll buy her share from you."

He didn't bother to wait on a response. He didn't care what they said and he didn't need their approval.

He jumped in his Range Rover and headed toward Scarlet's.

FEAR RIPPED THROUGH Scarlet as the man pushed her onto the bed. The scent of cologne and chewing gum hit her.

Hugh.

She squirmed and pushed at his hands, and he

finally released her. But his heavy breathing rattled in the dark room as he towered over her.

God help me. It had never occurred to her that Hugh could be dangerous. "Why are you doing this? I thought we were friends."

"Because you know," he said, his voice accusatory.

"Know what?" she said, playing dumb.

She was on her own now. Joe was gone and so was Ray. She had to stall. Pray she could keep him calm and talk him out of doing anything irrational.

"That I burned that photo. That I smashed that damn doll." He paced in front her, swinging his hands. "But I did it because I love you."

"You scared me half to death out of love?" Scarlet said.

He stared at her, eyes wild. "I've always loved you. Ever since we were kids."

She struggled to recall what had happened to his parents. If she was correct, his father had stalked his mother after their divorce. He'd probably justified his obsessive behavior, claiming it was love.

"I wanted to protect you, to be the one to comfort you when Joe died." His voice rose to an unnatural level. "You were supposed to turn to me, not that blasted McCullen."

Scarlet bit her tongue to keep from defending Ray. Doing that would only agitate Hugh more.

"I'm sorry if I didn't pay you enough attention," Scarlet said, grappling for reason. "I've just had so much on my mind. Joe's passing, and then Pullman and his daughter, and little Corey."

"Who was there to help you through all that?" Hugh pounded his fist on his chest. "I was, Scarlet. I've always been there for you."

Yes he had. But she didn't feel the same attraction to him that she did toward Ray.

A loud knock echoed from the front, and she clenched the quilt as Hugh swung around. "Who the hell is that?"

"I don't know," Scarlet said.

"Probably that SOB McCullen." Hugh strode into the living room and Scarlet raced after him.

"Hugh, I'll get it."

But Hugh blocked her from the door, pulled a gun from his jacket and ordered her to be quiet.

"Scarlet, I know you're in there," Ray called. "Let me in."

Hugh pointed the gun at her. "Get rid of him," he ordered.

A tremor rippled through her, and she nodded.

She'd do anything to protect Ray.

Inhaling a calming breath, she inched her way to the door, but left the chain attached as she turned the bottom lock.

Ray's dark eyes met hers through the crack. "Scarlet," he said softly. "Please let me in."

She shook her head. "Not tonight, Ray, I'm tired."

"We have to talk about earlier… I'm sorry."

She had to get rid of him, fast. "There's nothing else to say." She grabbed the letter she'd written to him earlier and shoved it through the opening.

His fingers closed around it, his eyes questioning. "What is this?"

"It's goodbye, Ray."

Trembling, she slammed the door shut. She leaned against it breathing heavily as she looked into Hugh's troubled eyes.

A slow smile curved his mouth, and he feathered her hair from her cheek. "See, now, everything will be all right. You and I will be together just like it should have been all along."

RAY SKIMMED THE letter Scarlet had written. She was leaving town because he and his brothers had given her hell.

That wasn't what his father wanted.

It wasn't what he wanted, either.

He leaned against the door, debating on how to change her mind, but footsteps and voices echoed from inside.

Voices—not just Scarlet's.

A man. Had Pullman gotten out of jail?

He leaned against the door, straining to hear. They were arguing.

Scarlet had seemed nervous.

A yelp sounded inside, then something slammed against the wall and his instincts surged to life. Not bothering to question what he was doing, he jiggled the doorknob. Scarlet hadn't locked it, and it opened just enough for him to see her coworker.

He clutched Scarlet's arm trying to pull her toward the bedroom, but she was resisting.

Pure rage flooded Ray, and he rammed his shoulder against the door and knocked it open. Scarlet gasped and Hugh looked startled, then Ray caught the shiny glint of metal. Hugh had a gun.

"What's going on here?" Ray asked, debating on how best to approach the man.

"I thought you left," Hugh said. "Scarlet and I want to be alone, don't we?"

He tightened his grip on Scarlet's arm and she nodded, but she was trembling.

"If you want me to leave, you're going to have to put that gun down," Ray said.

Hugh gaped at the pistol as if he'd forgotten he was holding it. "I would never hurt Scarlet. I love her."

"If you love me, Hugh, then let me go," Scarlet said in a low voice.

Indecision played in Hugh's eyes. "You and I have been through so much, Scarlet. We belong together."

The man sounded delusional. Ray wanted to reach for his gun, but he couldn't take the chance. Instead he raised his hands in surrender.

"Seriously, man, I get what you're saying. Just put the gun on the counter, then I'll walk out."

"Please, listen to him, Hugh. I don't want you to get hurt."

Hugh narrowed his eyes at Ray as if he sensed a trap. "Leave first, then I'll put down the gun."

Ray shook his head. "Not going to happen."

Hugh raised the gun again. "You can't have her. She's mine."

Scarlet stepped in front of Ray, putting herself in between the men.

"Scarlet, move," Ray growled.

But she lifted that chin again. She was stubborn. "Shoot Ray and you have to shoot me," she said softly.

Hugh looked panicked. "Get out of the way, Scarlet."

Ray reached for her arm to pull her behind him, but she jerked away and turned to face Hugh, blocking him. "Hugh, you and I both grew up with violence around us. You hated the way your father treated your mother." Her voice was gentle. "You're not going to turn into him. I won't let you."

Ray had no idea what that meant, and he didn't want to.

Scarlet held out her hand, palm up. "Now, please. Give me the gun and we'll work this out."

Fear throbbed through Ray. But a second later,

Hugh handed her the gun. He broke down and began to cry, and she pulled him into her arms.

"I'm going to call his therapist," she said. "He must be off his meds."

Ray kept his eyes on Hugh. If he made one move, he'd shoot the sick jerk. "The only way he doesn't get locked up tonight is if he admits himself for treatment."

Hugh dropped his head into his hands and rocked himself back and forth. He seemed to disappear inside himself.

Scarlet patted his back in a comforting gesture and made a phone call. Ten minutes later, he drove Scarlet and Hugh to meet the man's therapist at the psychiatric ward where they admitted him.

When Scarlet was satisfied Hugh was settled, Ray drove Scarlet home. She looked wrung out, as if she needed someone to lift the weight of the world from her slender shoulders.

He wanted to be that someone.

"He's bipolar. I should have seen the signs that he was off his meds," she said as he walked her to the door.

Ray rubbed her arms up and down to soothe her. "Scarlet, it's not your job to save the world. You've had your hands full with your work and Pullman, and Bobby and Barbara." His brothers had also given her a hard time.

But that would stop. He'd made a stand tonight,

and he hoped they accepted his decision. That is, if Scarlet would have him.

Had he and his family hurt her too much for her to love him?

SCARLET'S NERVES WERE on the brink of shattering.

Ray stood at the door, lingering, making it even more difficult for her to say goodbye.

"Thanks for helping me tonight," Scarlet finally said. "I know you need to go back to Horseshoe Creek. Did Bobby or Barbara admit to setting the fire?"

"No, and that's the damnedest thing," Ray said. "Bobby confessed that he hired that thug to beat me up, but he wouldn't cop to the fires. If he and Barbara aren't responsible for them, that means our ranch and my family may still be in danger."

The thought of anyone attacking Ray terrified Scarlet. "Then you should go home."

As much as she wanted Ray right now, his brothers needed him more. They'd just buried their father and someone was trying to destroy their ranch, their home and their livelihood.

Her keys jangled in her hands as she unlocked the door and stepped inside.

But Ray stepped in behind her. "What about you, Scarlet?"

She turned to look at him. He was so close

he was touching her, his gaze boring into hers, probing.

"What do you need?" he asked in a raw whisper.

She needed him. But how could she ask him for love, when she and her adopted family had torn the McCullens apart?

Chapter Twenty-Four

Ray shuffled from foot to foot, his stomach churning. No woman had ever tied him in knots like this.

He couldn't even think straight.

Was she giving him the brush-off? Did she want him to leave her alone?

He couldn't blame her if she did. Except for his father, all the men in her life had disappointed her. His brothers hadn't exactly welcomed her into their lives. Bobby had resented her and tormented her. Even Hugh, her friend, had frightened her with his sick games.

And he…he hadn't jumped to her defense the way he should have back at the ranch.

He cleared his throat twice to make his voice work. "Scarlet—"

"Ray, go home where you belong. Make up with your brothers and put your family back together the way your father wanted."

He remembered the letter she'd written him, relinquishing her piece of land. "My father wanted you to have part of Horseshoe Creek, too."

Scarlet's face twisted in pain. "You have no idea how much that means to me, Ray. I loved your father, mistakes and all." Her lower lip quivered. "But there's no way I can live on any part of the ranch and be your neighbor when you and your brothers don't want me there."

Ray's heart gave an odd pang. His father had made mistakes, but loving and caring for Scarlet hadn't been one of them. She might not have been born a McCullen, but she had earned her way into his father's heart.

And into his.

"You're right," he said, his voice firm. "I don't want you to be my neighbor."

Sadness tinged her beautiful eyes, but she nodded. "I understand."

"No, you don't." For the first time in his life, he let the bitterness toward his father go and allowed the love that he'd found fill his heart.

Scarlet blinked back tears. "Yes, I do, Ray."

"No, you don't." He pulled her up against him. "I don't want you to be my neighbor because I want you to be my wife."

A heartbeat of silence passed, then Scarlet's soft gasp. "What?"

"I love you," Ray said, as he gazed into her beautiful eyes. "I love you and I want to marry you and for us to build a home together on Horse-shoe Creek. And I want to volunteer at The Family Farm and continue what my father started there."

For a moment, she simply stared at him, her mind processing what he'd said. He loved her. He wanted to help her at the children's home.

He wanted to marry her…

As his words sank in, her frown faded into a smile, and she clasped her hands around his neck. She would really be a McCullen and have the family she'd always dreamed of. "I love you, too, Ray."

He tilted his head, his lips a fraction of an inch away from hers. "Then you'll be my wife?"

Tears blurred her eyes.

"Scarlet?"

"Yes, I'll marry you, Ray. I love you with all my heart." She stood on tiptoe and kissed him with all the passion in her soul.

Ray twirled her around, then carried her straight to bed. Frantic to touch each other, they tore at each other's clothes, lips melding, bodies gliding, passion bursting between them as they made love.

For tonight, nothing mattered except that together they had found each other.

Maybe his father had known all along that Scarlet was meant to be in the family. Maybe even that she was meant to be with him.

Epilogue

Two weeks later

Deputy Roan Whitefeather couldn't believe he'd been invited to the McCullen ranch for Ray McCullen's wedding to Scarlet Lovett. Guitar music strummed as Scarlet stepped under the gazebo by the creek to join with Ray.

Roan didn't belong here.

But he knew more about this family than they knew about themselves.

Knew Joe had more secrets that would rattle the brothers even more than finding out about Barbara and Bobby Lowman.

Maddox, Brett and Ray had already started rebuilding the main farmhouse where Maddox and Rose would live. Brett and Willow's house was almost finished and ready to move in.

Ray had drawn up plans for himself and his

new wife, and they were temporarily living in the cabin Joe McCullen had left Scarlet.

Hugh was in treatment at the psychiatric ward. Evidence had proven that he had given Scarlet the burned photo and that he'd smashed the doll.

The brothers were still grieving, but seemed to have mended fences among themselves. They had found a website on Barbara's computer where she'd researched how to cut brake lines, and used it to push Barbara for a confession. She claimed she'd only wanted to scare Scarlet. She and Bobby had pled out on lesser charges but would serve some time, and Bobby had agreed to rehab. One day they might win their way back into the McCullens' favor, but that would take time.

Whitefeather stood at the edge of the ceremony, studying the crowd, searching for anyone suspicious that might want to hurt the McCullens.

Maddox, Brett and Ray were determined to find out who'd set the fires. So far, the arson investigator hadn't found DNA to tie it to Romley or anyone else.

At this point, Romley was still missing, and they suspected he was connected to Arlis Bennett, but they needed proof.

He would find it, though. Just like he would find out the truth about how Joe had died.

The brothers hadn't questioned that their father's illness had killed him.

But *he* had.

And he wouldn't stop until he learned if Joe McCullen had really died of natural causes.

Or if he'd been murdered.

* * * * *

Look for the next exciting book in
Rita Herron's miniseries
THE HEROES OF HORSESHOE CREEK,
WARRIOR SON,
coming soon from Harlequin Intrigue!

LARGER-PRINT
BOOKS!

HARLEQUIN

Presents®

GET 2 FREE LARGER-PRINT
NOVELS PLUS 2 FREE GIFTS!

PASSION
GUARANTEED
SEDUCTION

YES! Please send me 2 FREE LARGER-PRINT Harlequin Presents® novels and my 2 FREE gifts (gifts are worth about $10). After receiving them, if I don't wish to receive any more books, I can return the shipping statement marked "cancel." If I don't cancel, I will receive 6 brand-new novels every month and be billed just $5.30 per book in the U.S. or $5.74 per book in Canada. That's a saving of at least 12% off the cover price! It's quite a bargain! Shipping and handling is just 50¢ per book in the U.S. and 75¢ per book in Canada.* I understand that accepting the 2 free books and gifts places me under no obligation to buy anything. I can always return a shipment and cancel at any time. Even if I never buy another book, the two free books and gifts are mine to keep forever.

176/376 HDN GHVY

Name	(PLEASE PRINT)	
Address		Apt. #
City	State/Prov.	Zip/Postal Code

Signature (if under 18, a parent or guardian must sign)

Mail to the **Reader Service:**
IN U.S.A.: P.O. Box 1867, Buffalo, NY 14240-1867
IN CANADA: P.O. Box 609, Fort Erie, Ontario L2A 5X3

**Are you a subscriber to Harlequin Presents® books
and want to receive the larger-print edition?
Call 1-800-873-8635 today or visit us at www.ReaderService.com.**

* Terms and prices subject to change without notice. Prices do not include applicable taxes. Sales tax applicable in N.Y. Canadian residents will be charged applicable taxes. Offer not valid in Quebec. This offer is limited to one order per household. Not valid for current subscribers to Harlequin Presents Larger-Print books. All orders subject to credit approval. Credit or debit balances in a customer's account(s) may be offset by any other outstanding balance owed by or to the customer. Please allow 4 to 6 weeks for delivery. Offer available while quantities last.

Your Privacy—The Reader Service is committed to protecting your privacy. Our Privacy Policy is available online at www.ReaderService.com or upon request from the Reader Service.

We make a portion of our mailing list available to reputable third parties that offer products we believe may interest you. If you prefer that we not exchange your name with third parties, or if you wish to clarify or modify your communication preferences, please visit us at www.ReaderService.com/consumerchoice or write to us at Reader Service Preference Service, P.O. Box 9062, Buffalo, NY 14240-9062. Include your complete name and address.

HPLP15

LARGER-PRINT BOOKS!
GET 2 FREE LARGER-PRINT NOVELS PLUS
2 FREE GIFTS!

❦HARLEQUIN

Romance

From the Heart, For the Heart